THE SOLSTICE PUDDING

WHEN HOLIDAYS ATTACK

ANGEL MARTINEZ

Edited by
JUDE DUNN

Illustrated by
CATHERINE DAIR

COPYRIGHT

Cover Artist: Catherine Dair
Editor: Jude Dunn

First Edition
THE SOLSTICE PUDDING © 2019 Angel Martinez
All Rights Reserved.
Published in the United States of America.

PUBLISHER
Mischief Corner Books, LLC

TABLE OF CONTENTS

Chapter 1	1
Chapter 2	25
Chapter 3	55
Chapter 4	81
Chapter 5	97
Dear Reader	113
You May Also Enjoy...	115
You May Also Enjoy...	117
You May Also Enjoy...	119
You May Also Enjoy...	121
About Angel Martinez	123
Also by Angel Martinez	125
About Mischief Corner Books	129

CHAPTER ONE

"WHY DON'T you just get her some nice jewelry like a normal person?" Miteg's voice drifted out from under the engine pod, his deck boots twisting and shuffling as he worked on a stubborn bolt.

Shandi smacked his soles with a mag wrench. "Have you *ever* seen her wear jewelry?"

"Well, no. But everyone appreciates a nice, shiny thing for a present." Miteg shoved his float dolly out from under the pod, blinking up at Shandi with his huge, orange eyes. "Don't they?"

"A lot of humans do, but not *all* of them. Unlike fekra."

Miteg shrugged with his topmost arms before shoving back under the pod. "It's a genetic thing. We can't help it."

"I'm not complaining, Teg. You're easy to buy presents for." Shandi went back to loosening bolts on the pod's top section. Her right arm gave an annoying creak as she bullied a stubborn bolt loose.

For now, it was just an annoyance, and she wasn't slowing down to let Miteg catch up to her. She might have a cybernetic limb advantage, but he had four arms. It was a matter of principle.

"Those wing studs you bought for my last Emergence Day were *krek*."

"I'm glad you liked them. But Major Sur doesn't have wings. She doesn't even wear ear studs."

After a suitable pause, in which Shandi could only assume Miteg was thinking about ear studs, he offered, "You know your elbow's squeaking. Want me to take a look at it?"

"No. Thanks, though. Pretty sure one of the micro-shocks is toast. I'll replace it later." Shandi removed the upper plate on the housing, revealing the fried regulator module. "There you are, bad thing. I found which one failed, Teg. Come on up."

"Thank night. That last bolt wasn't budging." Miteg scrambled to his feet, reached in with all four hands, and decoupled the module so he could lift it out. "Get her something else humans like, then. Why are you beating your brain against your skull about this, anyway? You're not family. You don't work together."

"Because it'll be solstice in a week where she comes from, and it's important." Shandi huffed as they wrestled the module over to the workbench. "And she's so beautiful and together and perfect."

"I see. It's a courting gift."

"No!" Shandi hit Miteg with a side-eye that should've been hard enough to knock him over. He didn't even notice. "Maybe a little. But mostly it's a solstice present."

Miteg's four hands made quick work of pulling replacement wires and data slims from the drawers. "If I were courting another fekra, I'd bring a crate of soft fibers."

"I'm kinda afraid to ask why."

"For nest building. Of course, they'd have to be really *good* fibers. All different kinds. You can't just put a pile of synth wool in a box and expect it not to be thrown back in your face."

"That'd be great if humans built nests."

Miteg poked her in the ribs with a gloved claw. "You should try. It's comforting and highly erotic."

She glared up at her assistant's black-furred face. "You're not helping, Teg. Seriously not helping."

They were silent for a few minutes while they pried out the worst of the melted, fused, and charred bits. It would save the customer money if they could repair it, but Shandi was leaning more and more toward replacing the whole pod. She had a reputation to uphold, her safety record better than any previous chief engineer for the station's small craft sector.

Not that Onwa Station's admin would fire her if she screwed up her perfect record. She was station-born. Station-born had the strongest union and were difficult to dislodge from their jobs. But she'd also been born to the job, toddling around her mother's workbench as soon as she could walk. It was a matter of pride, both personal and familial.

Finally, Miteg suggested, "Maybe an interesting biological thing."

Shandi narrowed her eyes at him. "I think you need to explain that. You better not be suggesting I wrap myself up in a bow."

He let out a soft *krekrekre* laugh. "No. Though that would be interesting. I meant because of her job. Something she hasn't seen before."

"Hmm. She does seem to like the littles in the quarantine nurseries. Maybe the fauna more than the flora. Like the tiny yima pups." Shandi glowered at Miteg's sharp-toothed grin. "Not that I've been stalking her. I just happen to go by Biological Customs on my way home."

Miteg's radar-dish ears swiveled in a fekra expression of skepticism. "Of course you do."

"But she's seen everything that comes through customs. I mean, it's not like I can just bring some unusual species on station without clearing it through her."

"Well, no. But you could be the one to present it to her. She'd still have to clear it." Miteg glanced around as if making certain they were alone. "I know a guy."

"No. Teg... *no.* If this is another one of your *from my data forger days* contacts—"

"He's not! That is, I knew him then. But no, Alain's legal."

Shandi rolled the thought around. Talking to the guy couldn't hurt, right? "Let's assume, for fun, that he's legit. Is he even in the sector? Does he always have unique things with him?"

"He's due in a couple of days and usually has something interesting aboard." Miteg grimaced as another connector disintegrated in his hands. "You ready to call time of death on this one?"

"Yeah. This would take weeks to refurb and end up costing more than three new pods. Why don't you call this Alain guy while I tell the customer the bad news?" Shandi stripped off her work gloves with a sigh. "They're gonna yell. But if they just came in for maintenance like they're supposed to, they'd save everyone all kinds of headaches."

"Not everyone's a good, responsible citizen like us, Chief." Miteg spread his arms in a preening wing flourish. "I'll see you in the morning."

Shandi put away tools and engine parts as Miteg skipped and flapped out of the repair bay. It was unnatural for fekra simply to *walk*, though they could in places where their bouncier mode of ground locomotion was impractical or a danger to others. Miteg, one of the springiest people she knew, had trouble even then.

This off cycle, she deserved a drink—or she would once she called the owner of that poorly maintained engine pod. Shandi winced in anticipation and sauntered to the comm station at the back of the repair bay. Get it over with. Get a drink. Go home. Stop worrying about what a certain Biological Customs officer thought of her.

TYRA AVOIDED crowded spaces whenever she could. Sitting in her regular seat at the bar in La Luna was different, though. The watering hole preferred by station residents, La Luna had fewer strange faces than other bars and restaurants on the commerce ring. She could sit at the corner of the main bar with a good view of the door, watching the ebb and flow of patrons, nodding to people who called greetings.

The work cycle had stretched into an eternal nightmare that day. People had been extra people-y. The wealthy shipping magnate who couldn't understand why she couldn't bring her unregistered mobile rock moss on station had screamed for hours. No amount of explaining the fragility of a closed-station environment had helped. Not to mention the merchant who tried to tell her that his Cygnate aubergine mice were the same as station service mice and therefore on the approved list.

Regulations existed for a reason. Biological regulations existed for incredibly important reasons, like everyone being able to keep breathing and not to die of recklessly introduced diseases. Tyra was proud of what she did, keeping everyone safe. But customs officers, honest ones of any sort, didn't tend to make friends. Station folk were *polite* to her. Oh yes. Didn't want to get on her bad side. But not comfortable around her. Not friends.

Most days, that was fine. Being alone wasn't a

hardship. Privacy, quiet, solitude—these were wonderful things. Close to Solstice, though... The family would be gathering, and once again, she wouldn't be there.

She sipped her horchata, nibbled at the vegetable chips the barkeep had slid down her way, and told herself she was turning into a sentimental old fool. The job was satisfying, the pay was great, her quarters were bigger than she'd ever had in the service, and hardly anyone ever shot at her anymore. Life was good.

Mostly. Melancholy had still tagged along for the past two weeks, interfering with focus and clear thinking like a toddler yanking on her sleeve.

Her thoughts had pulled her under so far that she didn't know someone had slid onto the stool next to her until they said, "Hey, Major Sur."

Tyra carefully did not startle and turned to find Shandi. *Good and bad.* "Hello, Chief Leavenworth. Long day?"

"Ha. The longest. You?" Shandi reached across to snag a beet chip, her shoulder brushing against Tyra's.

Moving away would be awkward. Stay where you are. Try for a little smile. "Yes. Long. Mine, too, I mean. The day." *Gah.*

Shandi's brows drew in as she waved to Tyra's drink. "You're drinking horchata, and you usually don't unless it's been a bad day. Not that you couldn't drink it any other day. I like it, too." She waved at the barkeep. "Hey, Tika! Can I get an horchata and whatever stew you have up tonight?" Without taking a breath, she turned back to Tyra. "Do you want one, too? Aren't you eating? You should eat."

"I needed to unwind first." *Better. Completely normal.* "I'll have something later." Before Tyra could stop herself, she'd downed her drink and stood, preparing to flee. Staying would have been better on all counts, but there Shandi sat in all her petite glory, with her cute grin and her beautiful copper skin and her buzz-cut red hair—and Tyra couldn't think of a single topic of normal conversation. *Don't be weird. Don't be weird.* She patted Shandi's shoulder. "Have a better evening, Chief. I'll see you."

The *Goodnight, Major* that drifted after her sounded a little bewildered. Tyra didn't blame her one bit. A hundred better exit lines occurred to Tyra before she reached her quarters, where she hung up her uniform jacket and kicked off her boots with a heavy sigh. Shandi never had trouble stringing more than two sentences together. Maybe someday? Definitely someday, Tyra would find the courage to simply sit and listen.

That particular evening it was protein bars and a planetary settlers' serial she'd started a few weeks before. This one was good, with lots of action and suspense that didn't involve explosions and firearms, perfect for distracting her from stray memories and from thinking about dark, dancing eyes.

"AND THEN WHAT DID YOU SAY?" Miteg was quivering, his fur bristling with held-in laughter.

"I told her she should eat." Shandi banged her head on the workbench with a wretched moan. "A grown, retired Marine, and I told her to eat like she was a toddler. My gods—of course she walked away."

Krekre krekrekre. The laughter got away from Miteg, slipping out in sharp little flurries. "Sorry. I'm sorry."

"Nah. It's fine. She was nice about it like she always is. So cool and calm while I just babbled like I was twelve and on my first crush." Shandi heaved a sharp breath through her nose. "Did you talk to your guy?"

Miteg flicked an ear at her. "He's docked. Doesn't have to launch out again until late this off cycle coming up. And he says he has a thing that might work."

Your guy has a thing. Shandi stifled a snicker. "You'll come with me?"

"Of course." Two sets of furred arms plus the wing webbing between wrapped around her. "That's what friends do."

"Thanks. Now stop smothering me. We have stuff to do."

Stuff ended up including replacing the entire engine pod for that idiot who couldn't maintain his regulator modules, running diagnostics on an Endovan shuttle's inertial dampeners, and telling a young xik that, no, Shandi did *not* have the parts in stock to replace their fried control panel right that second. The xik's antennae had drooped, and they'd shuffled off after placing the order, probably to explain to their parental group why they would be late getting home.

Poor kid.

The shuttle took the biggest chunk out of the work cycle, since the Endovans used a proprietary gel in their dampeners, and of course a hairline crack in the housing had caused the super-special secret gel to leak. The captain of the shuttle's cargo ship had played the *but what if we* game with Shandi for nearly an hour before conceding that he would have to send for replacement fluid from his parent company. That would teach him to cut corners and not keep the right replacement fluids on board.

When they were packing up for the day, Miteg aimed a little grumble-growl at his message center. "Our window's closing fast here, Chief. Alain's just been bumped up in the launch schedule. He has to be out of dock in an hour."

"No worries. We're done here." Shandi tapped off the systems still up and running.

"Inventory updates?"

"I'll do them from my quarters later."

Miteg's upturned nose crinkled. "You promised you wouldn't work after hours anymore."

"It never takes long. Don't flap at me like that." Shandi pulled on her jacket and took him by a lower hand to drag him behind her. "C'mon. Clock's running."

It was a short jog, since Alain's runabout was

only six berths down from the repair bay. The ship, on first perusal, did not inspire confidence. The loading ramp, pitted and pocked, listed noticeably to the left and probably required manhandling into locking position before launch. The outer hull bore the usual scarring of a long life in the black, but most ship owners at least tried to repaint the registration from time to time. This ship might have sported an *O* or maybe a *Q* and the possible remains of a *4*, but those were the only concessions to showing full reg.

A shudder slithered up the ramp when Miteg put his boot on it. He spread his wing membranes for balance and called into the open hold, "Alain? You aboard?"

"Hoy, Teg! Come up! Watch the loose plating at the top of the ramp!"

The voice sounded cheerful and friendly. Alain must have been simply short of funds and definitely not a pirate. Probably. Shandi kept a grip on the back of Miteg's vest on their wobbly journey up the ramp. With four hands, he had twice the possibility of catching himself. The ramp spilled out into a small hold, serviceable, if a bit dented and scratched around the edges, and at the top of the hold ladder stood a perfectly normal cargo captain. In gray coveralls and deck boots, he was average height and build, with skin a deep mahogany and hair clipped short to better fit a pilot's comm headset.

"Teg!" Open arms and a completely not-piratical smile greeted them. "And this must be Chief Leavenworth! Good to meet you."

Alain, since this had to be him, lifted Miteg in a bone-creaking hug, then surprised Shandi with a gentler one. "Er, hi. Nice to meet you, too."

His attention swiveled between them as he set her back. "Our Teg tells me you're looking for a gift pet."

Our Teg? "Maybe. Something station-safe. But not too boring. Different. And, um, cute."

"I see. Nothing specific, then." Alain's chuckle was soft and self-deprecating. "I don't have a lot of stock with me right now. But I might just have something? Over this way."

He led them to a retina-locked cabinet under the stairs and opened the doors to reveal a single bio-container less than half a meter square. From the ventilation panel came soft cheeping. A bird? A baby rodent of some kind? It sounded so small and sad. The peeps increased as Alain set a hand on the box and opened the lid.

"This is an ussi from Messier 302." Something climbed onto his hand, and he held it out to display the creature, a tiny ball of spiky fur no bigger than his palm. When Shandi leaned closer, she spotted two black eyes under the fur and several sets of tiny black feet.

"I thought Messier 302 had no fauna?" she said as she fought falling in instant love with this peeping bit of fluff.

Alain tipped the creature into her palm, where it stared at her expectantly, patting at her hand with several feet, as if making certain Shandi was solid enough to stand on.

"All the surveys said so until one of them found these little cuties purely by accident. They're temperature-resistant, drought-resistant, and can apparently survive for months without food. Not that I recommend testing any of those claims."

Snuffling sounded near Shandi's ear—Miteg sniffing at the little mite. "Are they smart, Alain? Like service rats?"

"No idea." An uncomfortable hitch caught on Alain's laugh. "I suppose they could be. They're very rare, though. Not much in the way of studies on them."

"Do they get bigger? What do they eat?" Shandi's battle to remain skeptical was a lost cause as the ussi nuzzled at the base of her thumb. The fur was so soft and warm.

Alain spread his hands in a helpless gesture. "I wish I had a *Care and Feeding of Your Ussi* manual to give you. But there's not a lot of info about them. I've never seen one bigger than, say, a cat, and so far, this little one seems happy to eat anything organic." He searched through drawers until he found a particular box. "Here. Some broken-up kale chips. See if they'll eat one for you."

The little ussi had tucked their feet under and settled on Shandi's palm, vibrating in a soundless purr. She almost hated to disturb them, but she offered a thumbnail-sized piece. The ussi rocked back and forth, untucked their legs and pounced atop the chip. From beneath the fuzzy body came soft crunching and *nom* sounds, so Shandi reasoned the mouth was on the underside.

"So adorable," Miteg crooned as he stroked the fuzz with a careful claw. "What d'you think, Chief?"

Shandi tore her gaze away from the feeding ussi to find Alain watching her with a calculating sort of smile. "How much?"

"They are rare." Alain's expression molded into a thinking frown. "But this one *is* quite small, and there are too many things I can't tell you. I'd hate to charge you for rarity and then have the ussi not survive. Let's say one fifty?"

Haggling was more familiar territory. "There *are* a lot of question marks. I'll give you seventy five."

They haggled down to one ten, a little less than Shandi had set herself as a hard limit. Not too bad. In her palm, the ussi had folded their tiny legs and slept with black eyes shut tight. The little beastie was so heart-wrenchingly cute, Shandi had no trouble imagining Tyra falling hard in immediate pet love. Alain threw the carrier in with the price of the ussi, then shooed them out in a harried fashion. He *did* have a launch time coming up fast, he reminded them.

By the time they left the aging cargo ship, it was too far past work hours to take her new acquisition through customs. Taking the ussi directly into the habitat ring would set off alarms without a customs tag.

"Should be all right if I take her in through the

maintenance corridors, right? Take her over to customs closer to solstice?" Somehow, the ussi had become *her* in Shandi's mind, and she was looking to Miteg for confirmation of what was probably not the best idea. Neither of those things had much to do with logical thought processes.

"Sure. The ussi's in a closed carrier. Not like you're letting it run through the vents." Miteg petted the top of the container. "What harm could such a sweet little thing possibly do?"

Which sounded entirely sensible to Shandi, and was Miteg to the core—half bizarre pronouncements and half sound common sense. They said goodnight, and Miteg bounced off to the habitat ring while Shandi took to the maintenance corridors and ducts. This was one of those times when *small* worked to her advantage. Someone Tyra Sur's size wouldn't have been able to fit through most of the passages and around some of the tight bends.

She reached her quarters through a ceiling panel fifteen minutes later. This was her native station, and she had been proficient at sneaking through off-limits places before she'd turned ten. The ussi's container sat beside Shandi's console as she finished the inventory updates, but once done, she was restless. Shandi smiled at the tiny snores drifting up from the container. Slowly, moving carefully to prevent jostling, she placed the ussi into a wall cabinet where she would be safe and insulated from any loud sounds.

Her arm still needed servicing, so she

unfastened it, setting it in her lap to replace the burned-out micro-shock. Various fluid checks and cleaning of this and that later, and she was still restless. She popped the arm back on, the mag fasteners mating with a satisfying click, grabbed her jacket, and left her quarters to head to La Luna.

Skipped dinner again, so might as well, right?

Food was the excuse, but the real reason? The one she was trying hard not to think about in case of disappointment? Well, there she was in her regular seat. Everything was aligning perfectly that evening. As usual, Tyra was alone, contained, and looking like she was ready to go off to work for the day. *Major Tyra Sur, Never Disheveled* might as well have been the plaque on her office door. In another place, another time in human history, Shandi could have pictured her as a warrior queen, those broad shoulders and big hands meant to wield a sword, that long aquiline nose and those deep, dark eyes perfect for staring people down.

Shandi dredged up her courage and her smile, waved to Tyra as she crossed the room, and climbed onto the barstool beside her. "Hey again, Major Sur. We have to stop meeting like this." *No, that's not what I meant to say. Erg. Please don't say, 'yes, you're right' and walk out.*

But Tyra just chuckled and sipped her drink. "Evening, Chief. Work keep you late?"

"Why, um, why would you say that?" *Don't act guilty. Nothing to be guilty about.*

"You usually come in earlier for your dinner."

She knows what time I usually have dinner here?
"Oh, yeah. I got a little caught up in things today."
Shandi dug into her sad little store of Tyra Sur
information, searching for a topic of actual
conversation. Tyra sat quietly, staring out over the
bar crowd, her back straight, long black hair pulled
back in a precise, stern queue. "You were military,
right? What brought you to Onwa?"

"The job offer."

Don't push too hard. Maybe this is a sore spot.
"Well, sure, but you must've had lots of them when
you left the service."

"Hmm. A few."

Shandi thought that was all she was getting and
was brain scrambling for a new topic when Tyra
went on.

"I was the biohazard officer for my unit. Hoplite
Marines. After the Sergian conflict, I... There was a
medical discharge. I wanted someplace stable and
quiet."

"Has it been?"

Tyra raised a black eyebrow. "Has it been
what?"

"Stable and quiet."

"Mostly, yes. Except for the odd, entitled
wealthy spacer."

"Ha!" The laugh got away from Shandi before
she could pull on its leash. "Heh. I get that. Always
someone who thinks they're special."

"Hmm."

Aargh. We were having a conversation! Don't let

it die. "So... medical discharge. You have cybernetics like me?"

That soft, low chuckle came again, half-muffled as Tyra sipped. "Nothing so impressive. Sure, I have some poly replacement where bones shattered here and there. We all probably did. I could've stayed in if it'd been a cybernetic limb replacement. A marine's *enhanced* with those."

"Oh." The most sentences Shandi had ever heard Tyra say to anyone, and they'd not been happy ones. Not at all. Every social cue screamed for a sharp turn in conversation. "Ah... can I buy you dinner?"

The eyebrow that had never quite returned to start position arched higher. "Is this a friendly offer or something else, Chief?"

"Friendly for now, with the understanding that I'm interested? And Shandi, please?"

Tyra didn't laugh or look horrified, both good things. "Fair." After they'd placed their food orders, she restarted the conversation herself, much to Shandi's relief. "Your arm. Choice or accident, replacing your organic one?"

She cringed at the end of the question, and Shandi could only assume she thought she was prying.

"No, it's okay. Accident when I was little. The whole *don't go near the auto-lathe while it's running* translating into three-year-old me definitely needing to see it up close." Shandi clicked the fingers of her cybernetic hand, staring back at memories that were more adult retellings than actual recollection.

"Luckily Mom was just a frantic leap away, or I might've needed a cybernetic head."

"Gruesome thought."

"Heh. Sorry." Shandi took a moment for a deep, appreciative sniff of the chicken protein gumbo Tika set in front of them. "They tried to do a regrow. Didn't take. And since I was still growing, I couldn't have a *permanent* arm. Mom let me try different things. I like this model best."

Tyra nodded. "Practical. Durable. Certainly a handsome arm."

Heat climbed up Shandi's face to nestle in her ears, which, damn it, was the only part of her that really blushed. She ignored it and smiled through her pleased embarrassment. "Thanks. It's stronger than the organic one. Real handy at work."

A snicker—an actual *snicker*—came from Major Tyra Sur.

"What...? Oh. Ha. Punny."

Shandi tucked into her gumbo, gratified when her companion did the same, and conversation gave way to polite slurps and chewing for a few minutes. Apparently, they'd both been famished. Tyra's reaction to the arm—relieved wasn't the half of it. Sometimes, dirt-born folks had strange ideas about prosthetics, especially fully functional ones, and Shandi had no idea what beliefs people held on Mar Esmeralda. Beautiful planet, by all accounts. Nearly ninety percent ocean. Beyond that, she didn't know half what she should if she was thinking of courting someone from there.

Conversation edged into nearly comfortable after that, even if Shandi held up the heavy end for the rest of the meal, telling funny work stories and kvetching about clients. Beyond quick flicks of her eyes every time someone entered or left the bar, Tyra stayed engaged and apparently entertained. *Excellent.*

No rushing, though. The major was a reserved and private person. Moving too fast risked scaring her off. She did walk Tyra to her quarters, though, incidentally, more or less, on the way to Shandi's. They strolled side by side as the corridors and foot traffic permitted, conversation turning in fits and starts to the next work cycle and the quality of quarters on station.

Tyra stopped in front of a door. "This is me."

"Aha! My plan worked." Shandi rubbed her hands together, miming evil glee. "Now I know where you live."

"I think you probably already knew."

Shandi shrugged. "So busted. There's only so many permanent quarters. That's why I repair ships and don't hire myself out as an evil genius."

Tyra rewarded her with a soft laugh, warm and velvet wrapped. "Thank you. I enjoyed myself this evening."

She sounded surprised to admit that, which made Shandi wonder. Was it enjoying time with Shandi that had caught her off guard or was it enjoying herself at all? If it was the second one, that was just too sad.

Without letting herself overthink, Shandi reached over and twined their fingers together. "I enjoyed it, too." When Tyra didn't pull away, just stayed there with her serious, earnest gaze focused on Shandi, she dared a bit more. "Would you mind... that is... could I...?"

As she dithered, they both leaned in as if each of her hesitant words ratcheted them closer. When they were a breath apart, Tyra whispered, "I don't mind at all."

Shandi stood on tiptoes to meet her, their lips brushing first in mute query, then pressing closer in soft, teasing touches. One of Tyra's hands—nearly twice the size of Shandi's—landed on her shoulder, keeping her balanced and in place. Balance. Good idea. She took hold of Tyra's forearms and leaned into the kiss, drinking in soft lips caressing her own, letting it go on for far longer than she'd planned. A sound escaped Shandi—an unflattering mewl of frustration.

When Tyra backed off suddenly, blinking hard, she stared down at Shandi, dark eyes full of confusion. "I'm sorry."

"What? No! No no no no no no no." Shandi waved one hand over the other in frantic negation. "I've really wanted to kiss you. For a long time." She snapped her mouth shut, feeling the heat creep up her face. *Crud. That sounded super creepy.* "I didn't mean—"

Tyra gave a sharp nod and took a step away, her expression shuttered again, neutral and professional.

"Of course. Yes. Thank you. For dinner. For the company. Good night."

The door whisked open at the press of Tyra's thumb, and she moved fast for such a big woman. Shandi found herself alone in the hallway, staring at the closed door, before she could draw another breath.

"Wow. I screwed that up," she muttered to the plating in the hall. "I'm the worst."

But as she plodded toward her own quarters, she replayed the shifting of Tyra's eyes, the swift, efficient movements. Major Sur had *fled*. Quit the field. Opted for a strategic retreat. Maybe Shandi hadn't entirely screwed it up. Maybe... Tyra was *shy*.

The thought slapped Shandi so hard in the face she stopped in the middle of the corridor. A zesh chittered at her in annoyance, spiked ruff poofed out as they skittered pointedly around her. Major Tyra Sur, decorated, retired marine, supremely competent Biological Customs Officer, wasn't socially comfortable. What Shandi had seen as aloof and contained? Well, maybe she was misreading everything and Tyra really had been repulsed. But she never sat with anyone at the bar, never spoke to anyone, stood at the back of station staff meetings like a forbidding plascrete pillar.

Glass half full. Yes. Pessimism wasn't something Shandi could hold onto for long. She would assume that this—whatever had happened at Tyra's door— had been a social anxiety bump. On with the plan. It was looking better all the time.

GODS OF THE DEPTHS, what was that? Tyra leaned against her door with her eyes clamped shut. Pity that dying of embarrassment wasn't really an option. *It was a kiss, a nice kiss, one you asked for.*

Only to panic at the closeness, the sudden intimacy, the whirling tornado of sudden possibilities she wasn't ready to face. Just a kiss, but buried images had assaulted her, flying at her so fast she'd lost track of who and where.... And now Shandi was either offended or scared off.

"Just me and *Storm Planet* again," she grumbled as she took off her boots and hung up her jacket. "Probably always." With a sigh, she sank into the chair in front of the holo plate and tapped the program on, backing the timer up a few minutes since she'd fallen asleep in the middle of an episode the night before. "Maybe I need a pet."

Determined not to think about the disaster kiss in the hallway, Tyra settled in and focused on Captain Flint struggling to herd his settlers inside before the next oncoming killer hurricane.

And what was all that about a long time? Have I been missing cues again? Being alert but not paying attention? Tyra sighed, concentrating on slowing her heart rate and getting feeling back in her fingers. *Shandi is never going to speak to me again.*

CHAPTER TWO

"YEP, we're still on, little ussi," Shandi crooned as she took the ball of fluff out of its box to let it wobble around her desk space. Kale chips and tofu crumbs lay scattered about the surface so the little one could play at hunting food while Shandi checked schedules and deliveries for the day. "Tyra's gonna love you. I mean, who wouldn't? And everything'll be great."

Nam, the ussi agreed as it pounced atop a piece of kale chip.

"Are you bigger than last night?" Shandi tipped her head to take in several ussi angles. It was hard to say. "Let's get a baseline on you."

She pulled her laser caliper out of a cargo pocket and when the ussi pounced on a sizeable tofu crumb, pointed the instrument. Fine lines of light ran over the puffball while the ussi turned to watch in evident interest, so Shandi had to measure several times.

"Okay, nice, round six-centimeter diameter there. Now we can do a growth chart for you."

The ussi's answer was a definitive *crunch*, which sounded close enough to approval. Then she curled her tiny legs under her body and began to snore.

"Eat and sleep. Guess you are a baby still, like what's his face said." Had he said that? Maybe. He'd said they grew as big as cats, so Shandi had assumed. Not that it mattered. If the ussi was eating until she was full and sleeping it off, that meant she was happy, right?

Careful not to wake the little mite, Shandi scooped the ussi off the table and secured her in her box before leaving for work, whistling.

Miteg met her at the last cross-corridor before the repair bay. He was practically *walking*.

"You okay?" Shandi bumped her organic shoulder into him gently.

"Mmm. My mother triad sent me a care package. Five packets of striped grubs. Guess how many I ate."

"Five?"

An ominous gurgle emanated from Miteg's stomachs. "Yep."

"Why would you do that to yourself?"

"'Cause they're so good," Miteg groaned.

"I'm writing your moms to tell them not to send you so much at once. You have impulse issues." Shandi patted his upper arm. "Sure you should be at work? I can call in an extra hand from the freighter shipyard."

He gave one wing a vague flap. "No, it's fine. I'll feel better moving."

"You're going off shift at the first sign of you turning gray."

"Yes, Boss."

The workday didn't go too badly, leaving out Miteg's two desperate runs to the waste disposal unit. Since he was nearly himself again after the second trip, Shandi called it a win. After conducting a scheduled inspection on a military shuttle and letting an ecstatic xik youngster know his repair parts would be in the next work cycle, they were able to get to the day's accounting and inventory management without going past time.

"So... La Luna tonight?" Miteg asked as he shut down his screens.

Shandi squinted at him. "You're not actually hungry, are you?"

"Me? Eww. No." He managed a sharp-toothed smile. "But I saw you and Major Sur last night when I stopped in to grab a *refna* to go."

"No wonder you felt like twenty tons of crushed asteroid if you had that foul crud with your grub overdose." Shandi paused in the act of grabbing her jacket. "Wait. You were spying on me?"

Miteg huffed. "It wasn't spying. Just saw you there. Looking pretty cozy. How'd it go?"

"Great. Until I kissed her or she kissed me or something."

Krekre. Miteg's laugh was just short of exhausted. "How are you not sure?"

"I dunno. We were kissing, something happened, and then we weren't, and she looked... revolted? No, not that. Panicked? More like panicked, yeah."

"Chief. I can't believe you scared her off already."

Shandi blew out a slow breath, cheeks puffed. "I don't think I did. I *hope* I didn't. Teg, go home. You look like death on a float cart."

The snort without a cheeky comeback was confirmation enough, and she propelled Miteg's dragging steps out of the repair bay. He promised he would rest and not dig into the rest of the parental care package. She promised she would at least peek into La Luna.

They lived on a space station. An enclosed environment with a finite pool of regular interactions. Leaving things awkward with people one might see every day—well, frequently enough—made things uncomfortable. Led to bad blood. Always better to clear the air....

Helped to know what you were clearing the air over exactly.

La Luna's dinner crowd hadn't ramped up yet, giving Shandi a clear line of sight from the door to the bar, where Tyra's usual seat sat empty and neglected. Crud. It'd been worth a shot, anyway. Should she swing by Tyra's quarters to see if she was all right? Would that be creepy?

A throat cleared behind her, the voice hesitant. "Chief Leavenworth?"

Shandi tamped down hard on the sigh and conjured up a smile. *What happened to first names?*

TYRA HAD NEARLY DONE an emergency about face when she'd spotted Shandi in the hall. For five awful seconds she'd stood frozen with indecision, then she snorted at herself. Dropship runs under heavy fire had never paralyzed her. One not-so-tall engineer certainly shouldn't.

Except she does, and words run off where I can't find them.

It would've been great to be able to say it hadn't always been like this, to say she'd been full of confidence and swagger around attractive women before... before everything had gone wrong. That would've been a lie, though. Tyra's awkwardness wasn't new and had reached legendary status with her troops. Her marines had never interfered, not quite, but they had developed a habit of nudging beautiful women her way. There'd probably been some bets laid on how long she took to screw it up.

Scoundrels, the lot of them. *Gods of the deep, I miss them.*

At least she'd managed something of a hello?

"Major Sur." Shandi's eyebrows had flown ceiling-ward in surprise. "I was, um, I was actually looking for you."

Say something funny, something polite, anything —say something. "Oh?" *Brilliant. Just brilliant.*

Shandi straightened, expression serious. "I feel like I should apologize. No... no, that's wrong. Let me start again. I want to apologize. For last night. I made you uncomfortable, I think. It was clumsy and sudden and I should've asked, really asked, given you time, and—"

"No." Tyra held up a hand, trying to gather words. "It wasn't. You, that is. It wasn't you. You were fine." There. That didn't sound strange or unhinged, did it?

"All right. I think." Shandi's crinkled forehead said she wasn't convinced. "It was still too... something. And I'm sorry."

Me, too. Say something. Anything. "Hungry?"

"I could eat." Shandi's crooked grin suggested all wasn't quite lost. Yet.

Tyra started toward the bar, then hesitated with a wave toward the tables and the more isolated cubbies toward the back. "Would you rather...?"

"Nah." Shandi's grin had regained wattage. "It's not right in here if you're not at your spot."

Relief, and a niggle of guilt for that relief, fizzed in Tyra's stomach. She wanted to demonstrate that she wasn't a slave to routine, and on the other hand didn't feel up to breaking routine at all. *Grateful. We'll go with that.*

A Shandi monologue about the workday allowed Tyra to regroup, nodding and humming agreement in the right places until they'd settled and had that evening's curry in front of them. She nearly felt settled when Shandi went on a conversational assault.

"So tell me about planets."

Tyra choked down her bite of spicy sauce and carrot. "Planets?"

"Yes, you know. Those mostly spherical balls that orbit stars. I've never been on one."

"Ah. There's gravity." Tyra nearly kicked herself. Of course there was gravity. Stations had gravity. *Ships* had gravity. "And, um, day-night cycles. And weather."

"Not all planets have weather, though, right?" Shandi shoveled food in between questions as if afraid to miss a chance for the next one.

"Depends what you include. Temperature changes, yes." Tyra sipped at her water, suddenly uncomfortable with the sound of her own voice. "For clouds and front patterns—needs an atmosphere."

"What about your planet? Where you come from, I mean."

Tyra side-eyed her dinner companion. "Lots of questions, Chief."

"I'm curious. Always." Shandi held up both hands in a placating gesture. "Look, I've never been anywhere, okay? Not sure I'd like the idea of traveling through vacuum to get somewhere, honestly, but I still wonder what it's like, seeing places besides where you've spent your whole life."

That made some sense, though plenty of travel holos could have shown and explained more than Tyra ever could. She had to concede that even the best holos couldn't match firsthand experience. "Mar Esmeralda can be... extreme. Hurricane season is dangerous. Ice season is brutal."

Shandi blinked at her, shaking her head. "Why would anyone *live* there, then?"

"Also beautiful." *To pilot a crest skipper with the clouds catching fire at sunset, with the waves, the world moving under your feet. I can still feel it. I can... still.*

"Do you go back a lot?" Shandi's voice had quieted as she leaned closer, searching Tyra's face.

"No."

"No?"

Trying to connect with someone here—you have to do better than that. Tyra herded her curry around the plate for a few laps before answering. "It's good and bad going home. Nice to see everyone. Good to see familiar things. But it's like..." Tyra wasn't certain she had an analogy Shandi would understand. "Have you ever seen one of those ancient puzzles? The ones made of paper?"

Shandi nodded with encouraging enthusiasm. "Sure. On museum vids."

"Ah. Well. We used to have some back home." Tyra pulled in a long breath. "Going home feels like I'm a puzzle piece, except I've been left out in the rain. And got warped and swollen from the water."

"Oh." Shandi placed her fork down and covered Tyra's hand for a quick squeeze. "You feel like you don't fit right anymore."

"Right."

The swift downward spiral Tyra had expected while talking about something so personal didn't happen as she'd expected. She stared at the hand atop hers—the biological one, scarred here and there from years working with engine parts. Slowly, afraid in some absurd flight of imagination that the hand might flee, she turned her own until they clasped palm to palm. It was a wonderful hand, like the rest of Shandi —both strong and gentle, battered and capable.

"This is fine, you know." Shandi leaned forward farther, threatening her uniform jacket with curry stains. "If you just want to hold hands. I'm good with that."

No, that's not what I want. I've been alone for what feels like a century, and I want so much more, but I can't. What if it happens while we're... I just can't. "I... This is nice."

Shandi's smile, while still bright, shone softer as she gripped tighter. "Okay. Better. Much better."

For the second time, Shandi walked Tyra back to her quarters, and again they both hesitated at the door. She couldn't keep doing this, simply letting the anxiety build to small explosions without explanation. Shandi was *interested*, and the feeling was mutual. Stupid, stupid, stupid not to face things head on. If she scared Shandi off, well, then she did. Better now than later.

"Would you like to come in?" Tyra cringed at the sudden gravelly quality of her voice. "Not for, um... but I'd like to maybe say some things."

"Pretty sure I'm a good listener without an expectation of *um*." The corners of Shandi's eyes crinkled as she unleashed a full-force grin, but her hand on Tyra's arm was steady and comforting.

The whisper of dread at how her quarters would be perceived died as Shandi's gaze darted around the front room in bright-eyed curiosity. Spartan by home's standards, but apparently interesting enough for spacers, Tyra had managed a few colorful cushions on the standard-issue furniture and did have a few sculptures and stills of birds and ocean life from Mar Esmeralda.

Shandi stopped by a turquoise carving of a celestina ammonite, and ran a whisper-light touch over the shell. "How pretty."

"From the family. They sent it when I'd... When I came here." Tyra settled on the edge of the room's single chair, leaving the long sofa for Shandi. Socially comfortable wasn't a trait she'd ever claimed. Work situations with regulations and clear objectives? Not a problem. She could interact on those terms without a hitch. Social interactions where she'd always felt people made up their own rules? Never easy. Far harder now.

"Very cozy and neat. My place always feels like a disaster." Shandi flopped onto the center of the sofa, giving Tyra space but not projecting an air of avoidance. "Talk to me, Major. Something's eating at you. It doesn't take a genius to see that."

Tyra leaned forward with her elbows on her knees so she could studiously examine her boots. She hadn't told anyone this story since mandatory counseling. "My last command, I had a small company of specialists reporting to me. Crack bomb squad. Experts in bio and chemical weapons."

"Were you frontline personnel?" Shandi's grin had melted into a frown of concern.

"Depended on the situation. Of course, in the field, any location can become the front lines at any time. My team knew they were marines first, specialists second." A shiver ran up Tyra's side, and she concentrated on breathing slowly. "Hard, dangerous work sometimes. But I was proud of my unit, and my Lena was never far."

"Your Lena?" Shandi's voice barely rose to a whisper.

"Yes." *I can do this. Tell the story.* Tightening her fingers around each other, she forced herself to keep going. "One of our drop-ship pilots. The best."

"You were a couple."

While it wasn't a question, Tyra still answered. "Yes. We were going to register..." *Deep breath, another. One more.* "Yes. It was Sergia Three—"

"That was the last big battle, wasn't it?"

Tyra lifted her head and quirked an eyebrow. "Military history buff?"

"It wasn't *that* long ago," Shandi huffed. "And I do watch the news feeds sometimes."

"Of course. It seems longer sometimes. Sometimes it seems like no time at all." *The point, Sur. Concentrate.* "Lena did a hot-zone pickup of my unit. Command wanted us clear for an air strike. We should've been clear. Nearly made it back to the battleship in orbit. But we'd picked up a gods-cursed bouncer mine at the landing site."

"Those are illegal, aren't they?" Shandi's question was hesitant and unhappy.

"They are now. This one was on a long delay. We were on approach when it blew. Started us on a trajectory away from the docking bay. Breached the hull. We scrambled for oxygen. Lines were damaged. Got emergency plating over the hole, but most of the air had vented."

"Inscrutable gods... How did you survive?"

The question nearly did her in. They hadn't all survived. "We... I..." Tyra closed her eyes, fighting her heart's attempt at a speed record. Shandi's hand closed over hers again. The warmth helped. "I suited up and took a propulsion pack. My marines tried to talk me out of it. But we were out of options. I wasn't sending any of them out instead of me. Used the pack to nudge and reorient the drop ship. Point it back to docking radius, where the exterior grapples could hook on. We made it. I'd thought we all made it. Everyone hollering and cheering. But when we opened the pilot's canopy..."

"Lena?"

Tyra nodded, swallowing hard against the lump in her throat. "Lena was dead. She saw what I was doing. Saw the dropping O2 levels in the passenger compartment. Vented her oxygen to give me time to save everyone else."

"I'm sorry. Oh, Tyra." Shandi knelt beside her

and gathered Tyra close, where she shook and fought the memories trying to overwhelm her.

"They told me she was a hero," she whispered. "Like I didn't know."

"And that didn't help." Shandi held her tight, stroking her hair. "Medals and stuff after the fact. Why do they think that helps? I'm so sorry."

Tyra struggled free, though she kept a hand on Shandi's shoulder. The thousand-kilo weight on her chest made every breath a small victory, her vision fading in and out. *I will do this. I will. I'm almost through.* "When I pull back. Startle away. Withdraw. I'm seeing those things."

"So it really is you and not me." Shandi's attempt at a smile was crooked and wobbly, but Tyra appreciated the attempt. Any more sympathy would have sent her over the edge into a blubbering mess.

"Ha. Yes." Tyra heaved a shuddering sigh, grateful to expand her lungs as even that sad attempt at humor lifted some of the weight. "I haven't been with anyone. I don't know if I can. And I wanted you to know."

"Just so we're clear—you're saying that whatever this thing is we're doing, you can't do it?"

"No." Tyra took both of Shandi's hands, bio and mechanical, and leaned their foreheads together. "I'm saying I want to try. But it won't be... normal. And might not work."

"Oh, well. If that's all. Normal is for dirtsuckers who don't live in a multi-species, glorified tin can in space."

Tyra managed a snort, and Shandi stood, pulling them both up together. The support was nice, since her legs still shook. "I think I have to call it a night."

"I'll admit I'm disappointed, but I agree." After a quick hug, Shandi pulled back. "You look done. See you tomorrow?"

I should say no. End this before it gets too bad. "Yes."

Somehow Shandi's smile lingered long after the door had closed after her.

*

"I'M COMING. Hold on. Sorry I was gone so long." Shandi hurried across her quarters to the ussi box, which was rocking on its shelf, desperate peeps escaping in short bursts. *I left plenty of food. There's still water in the attached container. Maybe it just gets lonely?*

The catch proved harder to open than it should've been and she cussed through wrestling with it. When it finally popped, the ussi surged out and plopped on the desk, causing Shandi to yelp and jump back a step.

"Whoa. You've... wow. Look how *big* you are."

The ussi peeped and shook out its fuzz before trundling around the desktop in a less-frantic state.

Shandi measured and whistled in amazement. "You've doubled in size, little girl. And I see why you were so agitated. That box is too small now."

After she'd scattered food over the desk for ussi

crunching and shot some vid of adorable feedings noises to show Tyra later, Shandi dug into her odds-and-ends closet for building materials. Keeping in mind the *size of a cat* comment, she cobbled together an enclosure that would be comfortable for a full-grown ussi, just in case the doubling growth spurts continued every day. Twelve centimeters wasn't terribly big, but doubled every day? Best to be ready for all contingencies.

Had Alain neglected her during the flight? Had the ussi been starving and suddenly having enough food spurred the growth spurt? She'd have some choice words for Alain if she ever caught up to him again. For her part, the ussi—and Shandi had to resist naming her since that would be up to Tyra—decimated the offered food until, with a final *nam*, she tucked her legs under and fell asleep.

"Poor little mite. I'll make sure you have lots to eat." Shandi lined the new enclosure with an old coverall, put a pile of carrot slivers in one corner in case the ussi needed a night snack, lifted the sleeping fuzz ball in with great care, and shut the lid. "There. All safe and comfy."

In a way, it was good the tiny fluff was growing. Tyra wouldn't have to worry so much about crushing the ussi underfoot when present giving happened. Part of Shandi still wished she could've handed over an adorable tiny fluff for irresistibleness purposes. Oh, well. Slightly larger fluff was still deadly cute, and now that Shandi thought of it, would probably help Tyra. She didn't seem to have any animal companions, though she obviously loved them. Having an ussi to care for would probably be calming and distracting in bad memory moments, right?

It was perfect.

Shandi whistled as she got ready for bed, quite pleased with herself.

THE NEXT DAY felt brighter when Shandi got up, as if wondrous things could suddenly happen. She found herself whistling again as she made sure there was plenty of ussi food in the container for the work cycle. Growth had slowed during sleep, only an additional centimeter, but Shandi reasoned that only made sense since the ussi didn't eat in her sleep. With her domicile alert system zeroed in on the ussi's container, her quarters would ping her if the ussi showed any signs of distress while she was at work. She should have thought of that before.

Everything just kept brightening when Miteg bounced in for work, completely recovered from his striped grub disaster. Shandi narrowed her eyes. He might have been a little *too* bouncy.

"Did your moms send *gha* root, too?"

Miteg flashed sharp teeth in a manic grin. "I only had one it'll wear off soon I promise just give me something to do that doesn't need much finesse or lots of things and I'll get them done fast or I'll just run around the shop for an hour."

Shandi pointed to a container against the wall with a sigh. "Go clean and sort bolts until you can speak in separated sentences, Teg."

With an incoherent shriek of glee or pain, or maybe it was a fekra battle cry when skirmishing with bolts, Miteg swept down on the container. All four hands moved in a blur as he wiped metal free of grease and grime and began sorting into piles according to shape and size. It was a job she would usually have given to one of the assistants or the rare trainee they had float through the shop rather than her one journeyman mechanic, but it worked well in an emergency.

She really was going to have to write Miteg's moms about these packages. They meant well. They really did. And fekra moms tended to spoil their one-birth-in-twenty sons. Still...

To be fair, Miteg only took about an hour to calm down to the point of recognizable sentences and had all the good bolts put in the correct drawers and the stripped or broken ones down the reclamation chute before Shandi needed an extra pair of hands or two.

"How did it go?" Miteg asked as he helped her with a tricky bit of rewiring.

Shandi hissed as her finger caught on a sharp edge. "How did what go?"

"Last night. I know you. You'd have to see if you could fix things with Major Sur."

Shandi tightened the connection and straightened to stretch her back. "Right. I mean, yes.

It wasn't an enchanted evening or anything, but we talked. *She* talked."

"Really? You let her get a word in?"

"Funny." Shandi smacked him with the back of her hand. "She told me stuff about before. About being a marine. Gods-damned hero is what she is, Teg, not that she sees herself that way."

Miteg folded all four arms and leaned back against the engine housing. "*Hero* usually means there's some scary stories or some really bad ones."

"Yeah, not arguing. It explained some things."

"You can't leave me hanging like that!" Miteg flapped his wings with an exaggerated huff.

"Pretty sure I can. Not my story to tell." Shandi chewed on her bottom lip. "Teg, do you think once you've found that one big love of a lifetime—you think you could love anyone else?"

Miteg's ears radar dished, his eyes wide in astonishment. "You're asking a fekra *that*? Seriously?"

Fekra, whose various life bonds never include monogamous pair bonding. "Sorry."

"Eh. It's okay." Miteg flapped all four hands at her. "But I don't think most *humans* even believe in the one-true-love-in-a-lifetime thing they go on about in media. You lose each other all the time and find other partners."

"Not always. Mom never remarried after Dad died."

"Chief, she was a hundred-and-fifty something."

"What? There's an age limit?"

By now, they were both snickering, and things

felt... normal again. The abnormal hadn't registered before then, a low-grade not-normal ever since the meeting with Alain. But everything would be fine. Everything was fine—with the ussi, with Miteg, with Tyra. Things had gone a little off-kilter there, but the universe had righted itself.

Solstice was in a couple of days, and everything would be perfect.

Three hours before Shandi normally closed up shop, her domicile alert pinged her. She frowned at her comm and tapped into the system. The live vid showed her front room, her sofa, the table where she'd set the ussi's container....

The container that lay shattered in several dozen pieces.

"Oh, no." Shandi panned the camera, searching. Had the ussi grown so big? Grown so fast she'd broken through her container? "Teg, I have to go! It's an emergency."

"What's an emergency?"

"The ussi. She's gotten out and I don't see her." Shandi was already running for the door. "I have to go!"

"Chief!" The *fwp-fwp-thud* of a fekra flap-jumping followed her out into the corridors. He caught up to her by the second turn. "I'll help you look. Your quarters aren't that big. It'll be fine."

"Right. Right." Shandi careened around the corner and nearly ran over a sweeper bot. "Sorry!"

The little bot cube whirred at her in irritation and scurried on its way.

When they reached her door, Shandi held up a hand to stop Miteg. "Spread your wings and crouch down when I open the door. Just in case our fugitive tries to sneak out."

"Got it, Chief." Miteg's wing rings chimed softly as he got into position, his expression as serious as Shandi had ever seen him. "Ready."

Shandi hit the door pad and hurried in, head swiveling back and forth to catch any small movements. When the ussi didn't immediately appear to make a dash for it, Miteg stepped in after her and closed the door. She kept her attention near the floor, peering under and around furniture.

"Uh... Chief?" Miteg whispered.

"I'm a little busy, Teg. What is it?"

"You might want to look at this."

Shandi straightened from searching under the sofa and followed Miteg's pointing finger. It took her a moment to figure out what she was looking at, the sight was so shocking. A dark spot marred the wall above her desk. The spot was a *hole*. In her *wall*.

"Fucking gods," she gasped. Not only had something smashed through the wall, it was far too big to have been the ussi at its last measurements. "Okay. Before we panic, let's check the domicile recording."

Some spacers and especially planetary visitors objected to domicile recorders, but station folk understood their importance when hunting the cause of fires or other emergencies that could threaten the entire habitat ring. Besides, they were keyed to the occupant and needed station-command override for anyone else to view them.

She ran it back to the beginning of work shift, then ran the feed forward at twenty-four times normal while Miteg rested his head on her shoulder to watch with her. First hour showed all was well as the ussi's container stayed still and whole. The second hour, she slowed the feed as the container began to rock and jerk on the desk. When the container burst open and a shape emerged, both she and Miteg reared back in horror.

Something burst forth from the container—a shaggy, black thing of jagged edges and bristling menace. It turned what was presumably its head one way and another, maybe testing the air, then yawned to show rows of sharp, jagged teeth. Apparently satisfied with its surroundings, it rose up on six triangular legs and walked up the wall, where it butted its head against the poly-sheeting until it had created a hole large enough through which it could escape.

Which it did in a nightmare flurry of bristling fur and stalky legs.

"Oh no," Miteg whispered. "That thing must've eaten the poor ussi."

"Teg." Shandi swallowed hard, her voice cracking. "I think that thing *was* the ussi."

"Can we panic now?"

"Oh yeah. Definitely panic time."

MOST WORK SHIFTS were quiet routine of a sort. Tyra oversaw her team of three— one veterinarian, one botanist, and a lab tech—in caring for any life forms in the quarantine room, and answered requests for clearance of any flora or fauna new to station admin. Most calls had to do with visitors' pets and planetary foodstuffs not previously catalogued. The only excitement most days centered on owners who hadn't read the quarantine regs and refused to be parted from their darlings.

The last thing she expected on a particularly quiet day was a near-hysterical call from one of the station section chiefs.

"Tyra—Major Sur! It broke out. I know it was stupid and there's fines, whatever, but you have to come!" Shandi's image yelled above the holo pad. "It's loose somewhere!"

Tyra frowned at the image. "Chief, I need you to calm down. What broke out?"

"The ussi. Except it's not anymore. Maybe you should come down and see this?" Shandi concluded, her face radiating misery.

"I'll be right down."

Tyra took the time to grab her case and to tell her subordinates she was going out on a call. Shandi hadn't been making any sense. Station-born, she wouldn't have let anything both dangerous and contraband in. Would she? Not that Tyra knew her all that well, but Shandi had a reputation as a competent and conscientious section chief. It couldn't possibly be as bad as she seemed to think.

And what in the name of water gods is an ussi?

When she reached Shandi's quarters, Tyra found her and her journeyman mechanic in a miserable huddle around the domicile's holo viewer. She edged closer to watch the vid with them, a horrifying clip of *something* breaking out of a carrier and smashing through the wall. No one spoke as she examined the pieces of container and the hole in the poly-sheeting.

Tyra ran a hand over her face. "You brought that on station?"

"Yes—I mean no!" Shandi waved her hands in frantic negation. "It wasn't that when I brought it in."

"Maybe tell me from the start."

After a deep breath and two of her mechanic's four hands clamped on her shoulder, Shandi managed a respectable briefing concerning a trader who was going to have his docking permissions revoked as soon as humanly possible, an admittedly cute critter of uncertain origin, and its presumed metamorphosis into something more menacing. The fact that it had been meant as a solstice present for Tyra didn't make it better.

"The ussi was growing fast, but I had no idea." Shandi shook her head. "Alain didn't mention it, um, *evolving* as it grew."

I thought better of you, Shandi. That you were someone to trust. Now wasn't the time for recriminations, though. While the story spun out, Tyra had searched her databases for *ussi*. The thing didn't exist—not under that name. She crouched and let her gen-bot out of her case so it could crawl around in the wreckage, collecting samples for tracking. "Sounds like the seller made everything up to unload a dangerous species."

"You think?" Shandi muttered.

A tiny spark of anger lodged in Tyra's chest. "You don't get to play the injured party, Chief. This is a serious infraction."

Shandi heaved a tired sigh. "I'm sorry. It was just—"

"Hold that thought." Tyra held up a hand as her gen-bot chimed and climbed into her open case to interface with her tracker. "We need to find it. Before someone's hurt."

The fekra journeyman—what was his name? *Miteg*—bounced in place, wings shivering. "It eats biologicals. Did it eat anything meat-based? Will it eat *people?*"

"Don't want to find out." With the tracker set to display station schematics, Tyra frowned at the blinking red light. The creature was in the maintenance corridors, because of course it was. She tapped on her comm. "Dr. Emilia, hazard-4 fauna alert. Recommend all nonessentials on lockdown with monitoring."

Emilia's tiny image appeared concerned but calm. Good. "General alarms, Major?"

"Not yet. No panicking the residents. I want you on research." Tyra sent the before-and-after images she had of the creature. "Two life-cycle stages so far. Find me what this is."

"I'm on it. Should I send Tech Agitou to you?"

"Not yet. I'll let you know." Tyra closed the connection and turned to an extremely shaken and mortified Shandi. "Chief, nearest inroad to maintenance access?"

Shandi cleared her throat and pointed up to a ceiling panel above Tyra's head. "Through there."

Because of course it is.

۞

EASY TO IMAGINE Tyra in command of a marine company or a battalion or an army when she went into crisis mode. Gone was the laconic, withdrawn woman Shandi had been courting, replaced by someone competent and commanding who was probably closer to her true self. Or maybe she'd always been this way, her confidence only shining through in a bad spot.

Either way, her powerful frame had suddenly taken up space, and her eyes had flashed hard and determined—sex on hover pads. Despite her shame and near panic, Shandi had to suppress a sigh of longing as Tyra reached overhead without the help of a chair and lifted the ceiling panel away.

Wait. She was going to...

"I'm going with you!" Shandi blurted out.

"No. No civilians."

Tyra's hard, cold glare cleared up any remaining doubts. That was it. Shandi's absurd scheme had ruined everything and had turned a budding affection into contempt. Screwing up romances was a talent she'd unwittingly nurtured, but wrecking her chances this time somehow felt worse than usual. Even though her status in Tyra's eyes had been reduced from *potential partner* to *that idiot*, Shandi still wasn't going to let her go after the evolved ussi alone.

"Hate to bring this up, Major, but you're a civilian now, too. And I'm responsible for this clusterfuck. And I know these maintenance routes. *And* I'm small, and you can't fit everywhere."

"*Chief...*" Miteg began with an agitated flap but trailed off with a sigh.

"What?"

"Never mind. If I tell you not to do the thing, you're gonna do the thing."

Shandi squinted at him. "I won't do the thing just because you told me *not* to do the thing. Settle, Teg. I need you to send out to your contacts, the... legally challenged ones farther out from the core. Have a feeling Alain lied to us about everything except what the ussi eats." She turned and pointed to the now-open duct in her ceiling. "Can you even fit in there, Major?"

In answer, Tyra hooked her hands on the supports and pulled herself up in a jaw-dropping show of brute strength until her head and shoulders vanished into the ceiling. She hung there a moment, perfectly controlled and still, before she let herself drop. "No."

"See? You need me. And the ussi knows me, which could help." With a raised hand, Shandi warded off the stern warning she saw in Tyra's expression. Gods, what she'd give for the softer looks she earned over the past couple of days, but that was over. She'd ruined it and had exposed the station to a dangerous situation. While the first part was beyond fixing, she wasn't going to abdicate responsibility for the second. "Send your tracking telemetry to my comm. I'll take the ducts. You take the corridors. Teg can show you the nearest door. We'll herd it between us."

The glare became a scowl, but Shandi knew she had her. Tech Agitou was far wider than Tyra, and there were no small people in station security if Tyra wanted to call them in.

"Fine. Here." Tyra handed over a telescoping pole with a textile loop on one end. "Don't try to capture on your own. Keep your comm open."

She stomped out with Miteg in tow, and Shandi pulled over a chair so she could scramble up into the duct, heart in her throat, determination still driving her. *I have to make this right, whether Tyra ever talks to me again or not.*

⊙

JUST INSIDE THE MAINTENANCE CORRIDOR, Tyra stopped to orient herself. She'd halted Miteg with a warning about staying out before she shut the door firmly in his face.

Claustrophobic access ways were no place for a fekra.

The creature—most likely not called an ussi—had headed in-station. Good, since its trajectory took it away from vacuum-adjacent sections. Its destructive capabilities didn't need to be tested that way. Bad, since the concentration of inhabitants was greater that way. Shandi's explanation that it had eaten any organic matter she gave it did *not* give Tyra confidence about what would happen if it encountered people or pets. *There.* She had Shandi as a blue dot on her readout now, moving toward the swiftly moving red one. They both appeared to be navigating the duct system still.

This obviously wasn't Shandi's first time.

Not the moment for self-recrimination, but Tyra's stomach had executed a nauseating flip and drop. She'd trusted Shandi enough to confide in her, and here was obvious evidence that she wasn't always as aboveboard as she tried to appear. Dealings with probable smugglers. Extensive knowledge of clandestine routes. Harboring contraband.

Tyra jogged through the corridors to catch up to general area of the moving dots. She should've been more cautious, researched any potential love interest more thoroughly. Once again, her people-judging skills—barring Lena—had shown how bad they were. Now she'd probably have to file charges. Later, though. Dangerous fauna capture first, criminal proceedings after.

Laser focusing on one thing at a time would delay the inevitable heartache she didn't have time for. It was coming, though. *Later. Later. I thought we had something. I really thought it might be something wonderful. I'm an idiot, as usual.*

CHAPTER THREE

MITEG'S IMAGE POPPED UP, superimposed on the tracking schematics, "Chief, Major Sur, I've got good news and bad news."

"Hold that thought a couple, Teg," Shandi whispered into comm. "I almost have a visual of our runaway. She's trapped herself in a dead end up ahead."

"Hold position," Tyra broke into the connection. "I'm almost underneath you—" Shandi stomped down hard on the double entendre that threatened. "—Do *not* approach on your own."

"I'll do my best." *But what if the ussi approaches me?* Shandi kept that to herself, too, since Tyra probably would've heard it as a smartass remark. Still, she edged toward the turn to put herself in the junction so the ussi wouldn't be able to get past her.

Noises drifted around the corner—scrabbling and *ar-ar-ar-ar's* that sounded frustrated. Shandi shifted forward for a peek, and there, right at the end of the duct, the thing that had been the ussi dug furiously at the metal plating.

"There you are. Hey," Shandi offered softly as she eased into the junction, blocking as much of the only escape route with her body as she could.

The ussi let out a startled *yarp* and scrabbled around to face her, the triangular legs clicking against brushed metal. No ocular organs were readily visible, though the ussi still managed an air of watchfulness, its bristles moving in undulating waves, possibly sniffing the air. Slowly, Shandi put a hand in her pocket, grasped the protein bar she kept for emergency snacking, and pulled it out.

While Tyra had said not to approach, she was positive the ussi recognized her. It couldn't hurt to reestablish a bond while she waited for the major to find the nearest access panel, right?

"Here you go, little girl." *Not so little anymore. She's about a quarter my size now.* Shandi unwrapped the bar and held it out. "You've got to be hungry. Do you want some?"

Rustle-rustle. The bristles waved back and forth. The ussi showed sharp teeth and shifted from one pointed forefoot to the other. *Rustle-rustle.* She took a dainty step forward. *Rustle-rustle.*

"That's it. Good girl. You know I won't hurt you."

A panel just behind and to the right of the ussi moved aside. Shandi could just make out a catchpole held by an arm wearing Tyra's uniform jacket. *Careful... careful...*

The ussi edged closer, chattering softly, bristles

rustling. Another step. Another cautious halt. Another step.

"Come on, sweetie. You can do it."

Yarp! The sudden cry was so sharp and loud it startled Shandi into dropping the protein bar. The catchpole landed around what was probably the ussi's head. The ussi surged forward. The loop slipped off and the ussi grabbed the protein bar with a mid-leg and galloped straight at Shandi with an ear-splitting howl.

Those snapping rows of *teeth* headed straight for her.

An anguished cry came from the corridor below. "Shandi!"

"Gah!" Shandi flung up her arms and curled into a ball just in time for pointed feet to trample over her and leap off her head. She cracked an eye and glimpsed the ball of bristles escaping through the ductwork.

"Shandi?" Tyra had forced her head and shoulders through the access panel, eyes wide.

"'M okay."

An exasperated huff followed. "I told you not to make contact."

"Believe me..." Shandi sat up, rubbing her head. "The contact wasn't my idea. But the ussi got away."

Tyra surprised her with an amused snort. "For a certain definition of *away*. A space station is a closed system." With a few grunts, Tyra bulled her shoulders back through the opening. "Come down, Chief. Let's regroup."

"Can I tell you now?" Miteg's tiny holo image was back on comm.

Shandi dropped into the maintenance corridor beside Tyra. "Yes, Teg, sorry. What've you got?"

"I'm so sorry, Chief." Miteg was twisting all four of his hands.

"Me, too. Go on."

"Alain lied about *everything*."

Tyra let out a slow breath. "We've gathered that, Journeyman Miteg. Specifics?"

"I was just talking to the kltra ambassador—"

"*What?*" Shandi couldn't help the startled exclamation. "How?"

"Well, one of my zesh contacts said it sounded like a kltra home-world animal and my moms know the ambassador and they're in-sector now and their aid said they would talk to me and—"

"The point, Journeyman Miteg." Tyra cut him off gently but firmly.

"Right. Um. The ambassador was really pissed. They said this animal is a chep, and only approved kltra breeders are allowed to raise them."

"So not an ussi and not from Messier 302," Shandi said with a humorless snort.

"No. Not as such." Miteg's ears drooped, and Shandi felt bad for making him more miserable. This wasn't his fault, not really. "Anyway, the ambassador said it's a three-stage life cycle, each one progressively more dangerous. The one we have now is bitey and hungry but shouldn't be life-threatening."

"And the third stage?" Tyra's words had ominous weight to them.

"Hold on a sec. I'm sending a vid."

Miteg fussed with his comm until another image replaced his. In the vid, a... blob moved through the hallways of a grand kltra house. Its surface gleamed a stunning purple under the kltra solars, and it moved with a certain amoebic grace. Shandi held her breath as the blob moved toward a kltra child who had spilled a bowl of grain. The blob undulated over the grains, carefully moving part of its bulk aside to exclude the child, and when the shining mass moved on, all the grain had vanished.

Shandi blinked at the vid. "Oh. That doesn't look dangerous."

"Okay, keep in mind that's a *trained* chep." Miteg reappeared, shaking out his wings. "An untrained one will eat anything organic in its path."

A moment of silence let the potential horror of that thought seep through. Finally, Shandi whispered, "This could be really bad."

"Yes. It could." Tyra shook her head and glanced sideways at Shandi. "Thank you for the deadly omnivorous solstice pudding, Chief."

"I'm so sorry."

Miteg waved in the holo image. "The ambassador's sending a chep trainer on an emergency fast courier, but they don't think the trainer will get to us before the last metamorphosis."

"Of course." Tyra tapped her catchpole on the

floor absently. "Do we know how big it gets? And how small a space it can fit through?"

"I'm not great with kltra measurements, but it sounds like it'll get about two meters when it's all spread out and maybe a meter high when it bunches up." Miteg scratched fretfully behind his ear with his top-right claws. "As to spaces? It's *theff*, so who knows?"

Tyra's forehead wrinkled. "It's... what now?"

"*Theff*," Shandi repeated. "It's the fekra word for a non-Newtonian fluid or anything both liquid and solid."

"Hmm. Nonporous container, then. Dr. Emilia, did you get all that? Can you catch up when we have a carrier ready?" Tyra strode for the nearest junction when she received an affirmative, forcing Shandi to jog to keep up. "How long do we have?"

Miteg crinkled his already crinkled nose. "Until the last change? The ambassador says it depends how much it eats."

"I'd say not too long, then." Shandi had flipped back to tracking, watching the red blip's passage. "It's headed for the kitchens."

Tyra heaved a sigh. "Because of course it is."

☽

SINCE THE REGULAR hallways offered a straighter line than the twisting maintenance corridors, Tyra opted for a full-out run down the main route through the habitat ring. Every being who could scrambled out of her way, and those who couldn't, she dodged or leaped over. Behind her, Shandi's *sorry, excuse me, sorry* became fainter and fainter, but she didn't dare slow down.

If she could reach the hive of intercultural kitchens before the chep—

A screaming fekra in kitchen whites flew past her, the outer edge of his wing clipping Tyra's head. Two panicked zesh and a human followed, making the distressed noises unique to their respective species.

So much for getting there first and preventing panic.

"Admin, this is Major Sur. Full station alert. I repeat, full station alert. We have an unsecured small predator in the culinary sector."

"How the *hell* did that happen, Major?" the security duty officer bellowed back.

"Talk later, ma'am. On scene now."

A short sprint brought her to the kitchens' corridor, and all she had to do to find her target was to move against the steady stream of culinary workers running, hopping, and flying the other way, some of the larger workers carrying the smaller so they wouldn't be trampled. As she neared the majority human kitchen, a strange sound reached her.

Nam nam nam nam nam...

Tyra slowed, treading softly and holding up a warning hand when Shandi's running footsteps pounded up behind her.

Nam namnamnamnam ..

"What...?"

Without turning, Tyra waved her to silence. She eased around the doorway and found the source of the sounds. The former ussi, now chep, stood on the central counter where the staff had been working, its front feet planted firmly in a huge frittata, head down and devouring away. In other circumstances, Tyra would've told the chep to have at it, since the frittata was made with the odd egg substitute spacers favored. Unfortunately, every bite brought them closer to the pudding-of-doom transformation.

"This can't be good," Shandi murmured at Tyra's elbow.

"Agreed." The chep ignored them in favor of its feast, so Tyra went on. "Circle around the left of the counter. I'll take right. Find something to herd it with. *Don't* try to catch it."

Shandi gave her a thumbs-up and bent low to scurry around the several shorter counters between them and the chep. Along the way, she snagged one of the long-handled paddles used to stir industrial-sized pots. No hesitation. While anger still simmered in Tyra's brain, she couldn't help admiring Shandi's courage and her determination to make things right. Though maybe it was guilt. Hard to say.

Happily feasting away, the chep still ignored them. It might have been unaware of them, but Tyra wouldn't take that bet. She crept along, placing each step silently, moving fluidly and slowly. When she was in reach of the counter on one side and Shandi had closed in on the other, Tyra held up a hand and counted down by folding in her fingers. *Three... two... one!*

Paddle held at arm's length, Shandi surged forward as a distraction for the chep. As soon as it turned, Tyra sidled up beside it and slid the loop of the catchpole over what passed for a head without a neck or eyes. The chep let out a high-pitched shriek and backed frantically, trying to shake the loop. Tyra lunged with it, then let it have its way when it surged forward. The chep wasn't any larger than a beagle, so it was more a case of finessing the loop to keep it in place rather than hanging on by brute force.

"Dr. Emilia? Where are we with containment?" Tyra huffed out as the chep wriggled back again.

"On our way to you now, Major." Dr. Emilia's professional calm did wonders for Tyra's swiftly frazzling nerves.

"Good," Shandi muttered, brandishing her stirring paddle when the chep hopped sideways at her. "Stay with us, little girl. Just settle down."

For three long breaths, it appeared the chep recognized and responded to her voice as it quieted, front feet tapping an agitated rhythm on the countertop. It broke the relative silence with a cry so high-pitched and raucous Tyra thought her ears might be bleeding. The chep's next lunge was far stronger than its size should have allowed. It charged forward. Tyra tried to plant her feet. It hurtled off the countertop, yanked the pole from Tyra's hands, and jerked her forward to land with an undignified splat in the ravaged remains of the frittata.

Shandi made a stand in the doorway, trying to herd the chep back into the kitchen. It knocked her over without any apparent effort and raced off down the corridor.

"All right there, Chief?"

"Yeah. May need an ego transplant."

Tyra levered herself off the counter with a grunt. There would be some colorful bruises, but taking stock would have to come later as she spoke into her comm again. "Admin, I need the bulkhead dividers in this section down. Cut us off. Now."

"I can't do that without—"

"*Now*, damn it, or start losing personnel when this thing goes through metamorphosis again!"

The emergency lights flashed on—in several colors to accommodate varied photoreceptors—and the sirens began to wail. Panicked food-service workers had done the work of clearing most of the sector already, so the shouting and running feet were minimal as people scrambled to clear the lowering bulkhead doors.

It only took the six steps to the door to realize several sets of feet were running *toward* them as well.

"Major!"

"Chief!"

Then from Miteg and Dr. Emilia together, "Are you okay?"

The fekra mechanic bounded up to them from

one side of the corridor, and Tyra's team rushed to them from the other, Dr. Emilia in front, her tail high and fur spiked in agitation, with Clara Harmon, the botanist, and their lab assistant, Agitou, close behind, carrying a metal cube nearly the width of the corridor between them. If it had been the same mass with smaller dimensions, Agitou could've handled it alone, but he was only three feet high with arms to match.

Tyra pinched the bridge of her nose. "Didn't you —any of you—hear the evacuation sirens?"

The sirens cut off and Dr. Emilia's red-furred ears pricked up from where they'd been plastered flat against her head. "What do *you* think, Major? Don't bark. You needed the container, and it looks to me like you need assistance." She pointed at the frittata still stuck to Tyra's uniform.

"And I came to help." Miteg crossed all his arms with a stubborn lift of his chin.

Shandi let out an exasperated sound. "Teg, why? So you could be chep dinner?"

Miteg's defiant stance crumbled. "'Cause this is my fault."

"Oh Teg." Shandi reached up—and she had to reach *up* even with Miteg slouching—and took his face between her hands. "No. No, no, no. You had one person you trusted not to hurt you take advantage and another person you trusted to have some sense make some really stupid choices. This isn't your fault."

The hug she gave Miteg, so careful of his wing

membranes, dumped a few liters of cold water on the remainder of Tyra's anger. Stupid choices, yes. Not malicious ones. Shandi Leavenworth didn't have a malicious cell in her body—all too evident in how she tried to comfort someone she felt responsible for.

Tyra cleared her throat. "Chep."

"Right. Sorry." Shandi's ears reddened as she disentangled herself. "Let's see where the little miscreant's run off to."

Tyra joined her and Miteg in staring at the tracking schematic. The locked-down section included their current location in culinary and a few retail venues, including a small electronics shop, a polymer crafter, and a high-end clothing store that advertised its wares as *all organic*. Since the universe had decided on maximum chaos that day, the chep could only have picked one place.

"Your runaway has expensive tastes," Dr. Emilia deadpanned as she peered over Tyra's shoulder.

Clara clicked her tongue. "That was terrible, Doc. I don't even know you right now."

"I don't know." Agitou's sniff held worlds of scorn, though he'd obviously missed the pun as he continued, "Their stuff's pretty pretentious."

Dr. Emilia jogged to keep up as Tyra strode down the hall. "Humans and magachens don't appreciate subtle humor. What do you want us to do, Major?"

"Need to herd it. Keep it from the ducts. Especially if it's gone pudding, ah, non-Newtonian."

Tyra grimaced. Yes, the herding had gone so well last time, and now it would be dangerous even to touch the chep. "We need—"

She cut herself off and turned sharply into the next kitchen they passed. Her troops skidded and scrambled after her. A far more motley set of troops than she was accustomed to, but they possessed more far-ranging skill sets. They were going to fix this—all of it—from the chep disaster, to Shandi's good name in the community, to whatever was happening between them. All of it.

"Chief... Shandi, I need you to help everyone pick shields."

⟡

TYRA'S USE of her first name made Shandi's heart trip and stutter. The *deliberate* use of her first name, which fanned the one dying, remaining ember of hope. Despite Tyra's entirely justified anger, she'd dropped the frigid use of Shandi's title. *A chance. Maybe I still have a chance, and I better not screw this up.*

She understood perfectly well what Tyra was asking for: Shandi's expertise in material components to outfit everyone with nonporous ways to fend off a carnivorous pudding. A quick check of the layout and utensils confirmed this was the majority xik kitchen with lots of hard, cool surfaces and trays for making what Miteg called bug rollups. The xik word was a little hard on fekra throats.

"All right, everyone! If you can manhandle one easily, grab one of the stone rolling boards." Shandi stifled a snicker when Agitou seized the biggest stone board he could find. He held it without effort, so she really couldn't criticize. Miteg tried to imitate him and ended up putting his back down with exaggerated care. "Everybody else, grab one of the metal cooling trays. No, Doc, that's a bio-poly. The chep'll have that as a snack. The one with—yeah. Perfect."

Once Shandi had double-checked that everyone had an entirely inorganic shield, she turned to Tyra. "All set, Major. Is it still in the shop?"

"Yes." Tyra frowned at her tracking. "Hasn't moved much."

"Probably a lot of stock to eat through." Shandi offered a grin and got a dry harrumph that might have been amused. *Where there's a laugh, there's hope, right? Please, please let there still be hope. I'll never bend another rule again.*

Probably.

Tyra had managed to find one of the huge steel lids for the steaming basins, long and wide enough that it could've served as an actual shield in ancient Earth combat. "Everyone behind me when we go in. As long as the chep's still feeding, spread out and surround it. Doc, you're here with the container." Tyra pointed to a spot on the image of the shop just inside the door. "Agitou, up to the ceiling to block access to the vent. Shandi, here. Miteg, here. Clara, here."

Nods. Some *yes, ma'ams*. This wasn't reticent, communications-challenged, everyday Major Sur. This was Tyra completely in command mode, and Shandi suddenly found it much too warm in the kitchen. Confident, competent—one look, and that solid *presence* made Tyra someone to follow without question. Into hell. With a smile. Yes, ma'am, indeed.

If this had been a vid drama, there would have been the heavy thud of fight music in the background as they strode down the corridor behind Tyra. Maybe some slow motion going on. Even without the overproduced dramatics, something lifted in Shandi's chest, made her feel taller, more capable, just by following Tyra. This must have been how her marines had felt every mission.

They gathered around the doorway, craning over and around each other to spot the chep—an absurdly easy task. What they'd been afraid would happen, had. With its body gleaming a deep purple under the store's lights, the chep in its final growth stage had oozed halfway onto a shelf of decorative hats near the back of the store. A sign over the shelf announced *Certified Organically Engineered Leather*, which the chep appeared to appreciate, as one hat after another vanished with the soft *foomp foomp squish* of collapsing and liquefying headgear. Only clear, clean shelf appeared in the wake of the chep's passage.

Silently, Tyra directed them one by one to their appointed places, and Shandi hurried to her spot at the right side of the shop to cut off access to the changing rooms. She could just about spot the moment along the chep's path of destruction where it had undergone metamorphosis. From the shop entrance to the top of a display table, the chep had made *no* attempt at neat, mannerly eating. Scraps of cloth and inorganic fasteners strewn across the floor marked the mayhem of its passage. Atop that one table, which might have held shirts or underwear— who knew?—the nature of its trail changed abruptly. One end of the table had been wiped clean, nothing left behind but a sad cadre of gold sequins.

From there, it had abandoned the fixtures and eaten a path through the bio-poly carpet straight to the hat shelf.

Apparently, hats are extra delicious.

Soft scuffing noises came from overhead, and Shandi glanced up to find Agitou getting in position by the ceiling vent, his hands and feet with their tiny beta-keratin protrusions allowing him to adhere to walls and ceiling like an old Earth gecko. The bright shop lights weren't kind to his mottled gray-green complexion, but the way Agitou scowled, Shandi wasn't going to tell him that.

The chep didn't halt its fancy-hat decimation campaign, apparently unaware as everyone took their places. *Keep it corralled. Get it moving,* Tyra had murmured outside the door. Shandi crouched low with her shield, muscles vibrating with nervous anticipation.

Does it see? Hear? Sense its world through vibration?

Shandi cut her wandering thoughts off as Tyra snagged a steel display arm from a denuded coat rack and stepped in front of the chep. Still it ignored her as it moved along the shelf to the next unfortunate hat, a flat-topped conical design with scarlet feathers and what might have been chicken feet. A pseudopod standing in for a head rose from the front end of the chep and considered its next dish with the air of a connoisseur before it daintily plucked the chicken feet off first and consumed them.

"Young chep," Tyra spoke softly but with unmistakable authority. "I think you've had enough."

She thunked the end of her display arm onto the shelf, creating a barrier between the chep and the violated hat. The chep's lead pseudopod reared back, and though pseudopods couldn't normally convey emotions, this one looked mightily offended. As soon as space appeared between it and the shelf, Tyra plunked her shield between, causing the pseudopod to draw back and the bulk of the chep to collapse into a rough ovoid.

"Tyra?" Shandi ventured softly, concerned the chep would lunge, since Tyra was shielding the hats instead of herself.

"Everyone circle in." Tyra edged her boots back but otherwise stayed rock still. "Surround it. Herd it toward the container. Slow and steady, everyone."

Shandi held her shield low and out front, creeping forward a step at a time. Clara and Miteg echoed her while Tyra edged around behind her shield again, inching the chep back toward the door. Agitou stayed on the ceiling, shadowing them, maybe in case the chep could leap upward. Horrifying thought.

The chep sent out pseudopods in several directions at a time, its movements jerkier and faster every time it only encountered steel. They'd managed to move about three feet toward the container before the chep stopped moving forward in a roiling pudding of frustration. They needed to do something before it became frustrated enough to attack someone.

In a moment of inspiration, Shandi grabbed a garment off one of the uneaten racks. The holographic tag trumpeted the all-organic nature of the jacket in keeping with the rest of the stock. It was a fussy thing with an asymmetrical silhouette and lace points along the sleeve. Happily, it also had an odd brooch-like decoration of several yellow leather balls, and Shandi used her cybernetic arm to rip one off. With a prayer to the gods of weird culinary tastes, she tossed it into the aisle leading from the chep to the container.

The movement caught the chep's attention. A pseudopod quested out toward the leather delicacy, and the rest of its blob body followed. There were no more cute *nams* accompanying the chep falling on its food prey—just the rather distressing squish as it absorbed the ball.

Across the aisle, Tyra made a go-on gesture, and Shandi tore off a second ball, tossing it a little farther down the aisle. They were apparently yummy, since the chep hurried after it and blobbed over it before it had a chance to stop rolling.

Shandi risked a glance down at the jacket as she moved up with her shield in concert with the others. Two more balls and about six meters still between chep and container. Might just be enough. She tossed again, a little far to the right but still in the correct direction, and again the chep followed. Her knees were starting to complain about crouching so long to keep the shield near the floor, but they were getting close.

One more left.

Could she risk throwing it into the container? Shandi was confident she could make the throw since it was a big target, but would the chep follow that far?

Tyra had obviously been following Shandi's gaze. "Do it, Shandi."

Lining up for more of a bowling shot than a throw, Shandi wound her arm back and lobbed the final ball into the container, dead center. A single pseudopod leaned in that direction as if scenting, and the rest of the blob oozed forward another few centimeters. It was working. Agitou dropped from the ceiling to join the horseshoe-shaped shield barrier on Shandi's side as they herded the chep.

So close. Almost there....

A rattling crash came from across the room. Miteg, orange eyes wide as ship's portals, stood frozen where his wing had knocked over one of the standing fixtures still loaded with merchandise. The chep halted its forward progress. The single pseudopod turned in Miteg's direction. Shandi could practically hear every hair in the room stand on end, even those attached to clothes.

The chep *lunged*. It went from perfect stillness to a blur of motion, crashing into Miteg and his shield before anyone had a chance to react. Miteg toppled with a terrified wail, taking two more fixtures down with him.

"Teg! Get up! Hurry!" Shandi scrambled over merchandise and dangerous display pieces, desperate to get to him.

"My wings are tangled!" Miteg kicked frantically at the chep, now trying to engulf his boots. The boots themselves were inorganic, but if it could flow inside? *Fucking gods.*

Tyra reached him first by way of simply bulling aside anything in her path and turned her shield sideways in an attempt to push the chep off Miteg's feet. The strategy worked well—until it didn't. At first, the chep reared back as it had the first time Tyra blocked its progress. Apparently, the thing learned, though. After an agitated moment of sending out pseudopods in all directions, it refocused and oozed *around* the steel lid.

"Holy fucking night!" Miteg's voice wavered and squeaked as he yanked desperately on his trapped wing while using one of his free hands to fling expensive pants at the chep.

Those worked up to a point but obviously

weren't as delicious as hats or leather-jacket balls. Instead of stopping to finish the pants—striped, sparkly, some sort of polka-dot pattern rich people could probably name—the chep plowed through the pile, still intent on Miteg.

What had been a calm operation quickly turned into a frantic scramble. Everyone converged on Miteg, placing and readjusting shields to block the chep, who found more and more inventive ways to go around or through the gaps between. Miteg did his best to scrabble away along the floor, dragging the tangled fixtures with him, while Tyra manhandled the whole mess to reorient everyone into moving toward the container again.

The chep surged around Agitou. A meter-long pseudopod clamped onto Miteg's boot, and this time his screams were equal parts pain and terror. Shandi dropped her shield and dove for him, reaching into the chep with her cyber arm as she tried to separate his boot, now trapped under the chep, and his foot. With a shuddering cry, Miteg wrenched his foot free and curled into a ball as Shandi tried to de-chep her arm. It should have been easy. The little bastard wouldn't have had any interest in the titanium alloy carapace.

Except...

Sudden pain shot up the arm to Shandi's shoulder. "Ahh! Crap! It's oozed in to feed on the neural net!"

The largely organic neural net. Tyra's roar as she thudded to her knees beside Shandi was ferocious and a little frightening. She grabbed Shandi around the waist and heaved, trying to pull her free, but the chep just stretched to come with them.

"Detach the arm!" Tyra bellowed.

Shandi reached over with shaking fingers and tried to hit the release sequence. The agony in her arm made it impossible to focus. "I can't... I can't..." Her breath came in sobs. *What a horrible way to die.*

"Hold on, Chief. I got this." Miteg spoke in her ear, finally free of his display-rack prison. He hooked his claws under the joint, hit the right sensors in order, and popped the arm loose.

The sudden release sent the three of them sprawling one way as the chep's pseudopod snapped back in the opposite direction. The pain cut off immediately with the loss of the neural net, and Shandi landed on Tyra, which would've been nice under any other circumstances. Watching her favorite arm vanish into the purple chep gloop stabbed at Shandi's heart, but it was better than all of her being consumed.

With the sharp hunting cry of her people, Dr. Emilia ripped one of the longer, broader display shelves from the wall. "Agitou! Scoop and toss!"

Shandi had no idea what she meant. Luckily, Agitou knew precisely. He joined her with his stone shield, and together they shoved metal shelf and slab under the chep, lifted, and heaved. The chep experienced flight, sailing in shining purple glory for one second before it landed with a splat inside the container, where Clara slammed the door down and locked it.

The botanist hopped from one foot to the other, shaking her hands out with a little *eeeee.* "Let's never, ever do that again, Major."

"Everyone all right?" Tyra called out.

"Besides losing an arm? Sure." Shandi huffed, though she made no move to leave Tyra's embrace.

"Replaceable," Tyra countered without inflection.

"True. Teg?"

"I'm... no. Not really. Ow." Miteg cradled his bare foot in three hands.

Shandi scrambled over the detritus on the floor to reach him, carefully moving one of his hands to the side to check. The chep had denuded several patches of fur around his ankle, the skin underneath blistering and seeping dark fekra blood.

"You'll be okay, Teg." Shandi smoothed the crest of fur between his ears. *Please be okay. If that thing's saliva... digestive fluid—whatever—is poisonous...*

Dr. Emilia gently pushed everyone else aside and did the sensible thing, rinsing the affected areas with water from a bottle in her vet's bag. "Major, I think we're ready to call in, yes?"

For a long moment, Tyra stared at the container as if she expected the chep to seep through the impermeable box at any moment. "Yes." After a deep inhale, she tapped comm. "Admin, this is Major Sur. All clear. I repeat, all clear. I'll need Medical and

Maintenance to Madame Liliane's Boutique Pastorale in this sector."

"That's what the shop's called? Eww. It *is* pretentious." Miteg tugged on Shandi's remaining sleeve, his voice wavering as he pleaded, "Don't tell my moms about this, Chief."

"I won't, but you know Medical has to. Nothing I can do about that." Shandi patted his claws.

Reporting any legal or medical issues to his mother group was part of Teg's parole from his less-than-legitimate days after he ran away from home, and his moms used any excuse to try to guilt him back to the nest. In their minds, grown fekra males should be engaged in *sek*—essentially glorified stud services—and respectable professions like rock art or silk weaving. Ship mechanic was a job for females, they'd told him more than once, not delicate, precious males.

"Stupid legal stuff," Miteg muttered darkly.

Tyra stood, scrubbing both hands over her face. "Yes. Legal stuff. By rights, I should drag you both to a detention cell."

"I know, but—" Shandi tried to protest.

Tyra cut her off with a sharp gesture. "I'm trusting you not to run. Get Miteg settled at Medical. Sort out your arm." She turned a sharp gaze on Shandi. "You do *have* alternatives?"

"Yes." Shandi's voice sounded tinny and small in her ears.

"Good. Get sorted. Then come to my office. There will be consequences for this disaster."

"Yes, ma'am."

Shandi's heart sank to her feet and through several of the station decks below. That was it, then —the end of something beautiful before it had a chance to begin.

CHAPTER FOUR

"TRAFFIC CONTROL CONFIRMS the kltra trainer's inbound, ma'am. ETA, four hours."

Chep trainer. They're not training kltra. Tyra let the undiplomatic slip go and nodded to the admin tech. "Pronouns confirmed? Name?"

"Ummm." The tech tapped at his keyboard for a bit. "Kif pronouns. The manifest says Endra Fi."

"Thank you." Tyra closed the connection and leaned back in her office chair to stare at the chep's container by her desk. "Civilized, chep. That's what you'll be soon."

The container rattled as the chep flung itself about, either reacting to her voice or to the thought of being tamed. Who knew?

Her insides still shook, muscles twitching at odd moments. So far, she'd managed to hold off the episode that threatened by keeping busy. Maybe everything would settle. Maybe it wouldn't, but she could hold on by her fingernails a little longer.

Images kept flashing, though, no matter what she did. Shandi, brave and determined, hunkered behind her shield to herd the chep. Shandi leaping to save Miteg. Shandi's arm vanishing into the creature. Shandi... Lena...

Gods. Breathe. Count. Breathe.

Purple ooze creeping up Shandi's arm... The horror on her face...

Breathe!

Shandi's scream of pain.

Tyra put her forehead on the desk, the polyceramic cool against her skin. She was in her office. Compiling incoming reports. Taking irate phone calls from kitchen supervisors and one incandescently furious shop owner. This was her job, and Shandi was fine. Mostly. She'd lost that beautiful custom arm, but she was fine.

Her brain refused to believe it, since Shandi wasn't right in front of her.

Shining purple oozing up her arm...

"Hey, hey. You all right, there?" The voice, full of soft concern, and the hand laid gently on her arm broke through the loop. Shandi knelt by her chair, peering up at her.

"I... no." Tyra sat up, dizzy and shaking. "No."

Shandi hitched herself up on the desk and took Tyra's hand. "What can I do?"

"Just... wait with me. Talk."

Tyra squeezed her fingers. She reached for Shandi's other hand and stopped when she saw that this arm only had a grab claw instead of a fully functioning hand. Her hesitation obviously registered, as Shandi started to move it out of reach, but Tyra needed the anchor and grabbed it back.

"Well, okay, then." Shandi cleared her throat and shifted on the desk but didn't try to take either hand back. "I was kinda expecting to get read my list of crimes when I came, so I didn't have much conversation prepared."

At any other time, Tyra would have pointed out that Shandi never ran out of things to say, but she'd clamped her jaw too tightly.

"But Teg's doing okay. He'll have to spend a day in the infirmary under observation, since we're not sure what chep digestion actually *is*. Doesn't look too bad, though, all cleaned up. He's more worried about his moms. Who I talked to. Just to get them news firsthand so they didn't, ah, overreact. Too much. They fussed and yelled, but they didn't demand that their little boy come home. I guess they're learning."

"Learning?" Tyra forced out through the shudders.

"Yeah. That's why he ran away in the first place. They wouldn't take him seriously when he wanted to work on ships. And you can picture what happened—sheltered fekra boy gets scooped up by bad company. They exploited him for his mathematical talents. The crew eventually got caught, and Teg learned the basics of ships' mechanics during rehabilitation. He came to me after his apprenticeship and... well, his moms think of me as a big sister for him. They trust me as far as they can for a non-fekra." Shandi heaved a sigh heavy with anxious regret. "I let him down, Major. I'm supposed to watch out for him."

Tyra shook her head so hard she felt dizzy again. "You saved him."

"He shouldn't have been there." Shandi's smile twisted. "I should've sent him away. He's a good kid, stubborn sometimes, but he would've listened if I'd insisted."

"You can't be responsible for other's decisions." Tyra sat back to search Shandi's face. "At least that's what they kept telling me in therapy."

"Was that a terrible, self-deprecating joke, Major?" Shandi tipped her head to the side. "You seem steadier."

"Yes, thank you." Tyra shoved her chair back further and finally let go of Shandi's hands. She didn't want to, quite the opposite, and now that Shandi was here, she wanted to have a different conversation entirely than the one she had to have. *Professional. Concentrate on professional again.* "We should get to the official part of your visit."

Shandi heaved another sigh, this one leaning more toward drama than emotion, and flopped into the chair beside Tyra's desk. "Yeah, I'd rather not drag that part out. Am I being detained?"

To keep from staring at Shandi, Tyra glanced through the notes on her holoscreen. "No need for that. You've broken station regs but not interstellar laws except destruction of property. First offense. I have discretion on formal charges."

"I'm hearing a *however* coming up here." Shandi stretched out in her chair, compact legs crossed at the ankle.

"However, the station charges are substantial. Storage of contraband. Endangerment of personnel. Threat to station integrity."

Shandi clicked the digits of her grab claw in an unconscious way. "I'm scared to see the total on the fines, but I have savings."

"Hmm, yes. The fines are hefty." Tyra cringed as she pulled up the second set of numbers. "The reimbursements to the Kitchens Guild and to Madame Liliane's are worse."

She turned the screen to show Shandi, who paled and sank farther down on her chair. "Holy inscrutable gods. I can't... even with all my wages for the next two years..."

"They were very expensive hats."

"This isn't funny, Tyra."

"Simple truth." She turned the screen back so the astronomical numbers weren't glaring at Shandi. One side of her mouth quirked up. "Though you may be the first person ever charged with illegal possession of a murderous pudding."

"Hilarious." Shandi ran both hands, organic and not, over her short-cropped hair. "Will they take payments on it? How am I supposed to do this? I'll have to give up my apartment and move into crew barracks. And never, ever eat out again for the rest of my life. And not buy anything. And maybe mortgage some of the shop equipment." She dropped her hands to her lap and stared at them.

"You won't have the funds to replace your arm," Tyra ventured as the cause of her sudden silence.

"No," Shandi whispered.

The single anguished word stabbed Tyra through the heart. She rolled her chair around the desk where she could take up Shandi's hands again. "Listen. There are ways. I'm going to put the charges document together. You're going to sign it. Then you take it to Uwe Menotti in Life and Health Services. There's help. There's *assistance*. You don't have to do everything yourself. He'll help you negotiate and plan."

"Thanks." Shandi bent her head to wipe her eyes against her sleeve. "I thought you'd be really angry. Why aren't you angry? *I'm* mad at me, and it was me being dumb."

"I was. I am." Tyra gave her a little shake. "What an irresponsible thing to do. But it was... you made bad decisions because of me. I... I think you care. I know I do."

Shandi let out a hiccupping, watery laugh. "You were supposed to say that after I gave you the cutest fuzzy pet in the galaxy for Solstice. But, well, things kinda went off script there. I do care about you. Yeah, I've been creeping on you for a while. Sorry again. But it's different now. I think about you a *lot*. About seeing you again. What you're doing. Thinking. About when we can talk next. What we'd say. About trying for that kiss again, but when we're both ready."

Seeing Shandi so close to breaking down did messy things to Tyra's insides. This wasn't right. Shandi should've been smiling and teasing, talking a mile a minute, not struggling to get sentences out. With most people, Tyra would have felt uncomfortable, at a loss. With Shandi, it simply hurt to see, and she felt an urgent need to fix it, to erase all the guilt and pain from Shandi's eyes.

Moving slowly, Tyra reached up to cup Shandi's cheek and tip her head up. The moment's fragility made it hard to breathe. It felt as if any wrong movement, any word out of place, would cause the universe to crack.

"I think..." Tyra leaned closer, though not too close. Not yet. "I think I'm ready."

Shandi sniffed, but a smile blossomed on her lovely pixie face. "Yeah?"

"Yes."

In Tyra's mind, the whole thing had been graceful and beautiful. The reality was a little more awkward. They leaned the same way and both tried to adjust. Hands hung in the air, unsure where to land. Shandi snickered and placed one of Tyra's hands on her shoulder, the other at her waist. Then her grab claw took hold of Tyra's uniform jacket and pulled her forward.

"Relax, Major. It's just a kiss," Shandi whispered against her lips, the words sending little jolts down Tyra's spine.

Soft. Of course, her lips were soft, but there was also something exquisitely careful in Shandi's approach, each brush and press asking permission for more. Tyra slid her hands under Shandi's arms and lifted her, pulling Shandi's slight weight onto her lap.

"Yes," she whispered against kiss-darkened lips. "Yes to everything."

"Oooh, everything. Let's not get ahead of ourselves here." Shandi nipped at her jaw, then froze. "Um. Does your office door lock?"

"Good thinking." Tyra reached over to her desk without turning and hit the lock command.

"Thank the gods. I really didn't want Agitou walking in on us. Or Dr. Emilia. Scandalous. Or what if—mmph."

Tyra thought it best to cut off the stream of words with another kiss, letting her tongue tease at the seam of Shandi's lips. This wasn't professional, doing this in her office. Right then, she couldn't have cared any less. Shandi's tongue caressed hers, unhurried and thorough enough to turn all the little electric jolts into hungry warmth spreading up from her thighs.

There were flashes of Lena, of things that should never intrude on a moment like this. Of course there were. The kisses weren't magic. They wouldn't erase the past or suddenly make everything better. But Shandi's patience—whenever Tyra had to pull back and breathe through it— made all the difference. She waited, stroking Tyra's arms, giving her space until she returned to the moment.

The desire to run off and hide faded gradually into the background.

"I've always thought women in uniform were hot." Shandi pulled back, playing with the top button of Tyra's jacket.

Tyra managed not to snort. "That describes half the station staff."

"Oh, well, those. No, see, those women in admin and most of the ones in security? On them it's just work clothes. On you, the way you carry yourself, the way you move—on you it's a uniform."

"I see." Tyra reached up and snagged the pull of Shandi's zipper, slowly tugging it down tooth by tooth. It didn't reveal much, since Shandi wore a black T-shirt underneath, but one had to start somewhere. "Do you want it on?"

"The coverall? Hell, no." Shandi squirmed out of the sleeves to let the coverall pool around her hips.

"The uniform."

"Oh. Ha. How about on for now?"

Tyra nodded and lifted Shandi again to sit her atop the desk, tugging her coveralls down past her entirely too-adorable butt in the process. Underneath, Shandi wore boxer briefs of a vision-shattering neon green—both practical for the workday and full of mischief all at once. Couldn't have been more fitting.

"You look like a woman with a plan." Shandi squirmed in deliciously obvious anticipation.

Tyra halted her campaign to offer a little smile. "Never go in without one."

"Your eyes have sparks when you smile." Shandi's voice had gone soft and shy. "I like sparks."

The temptation to say something entirely too predictable about sparks was almost too much. Instead, Tyra lifted Shandi's T-shirt to kiss just above her navel. A sharp intake of breath rewarded Tyra, and she gripped both of Shandi's legs, running her thumbs along the seams of hip and thigh.

"You're really—" Shandi cut off when Tyra grasped the waistband of her briefs, lifting her hips obligingly as Tyra pulled them down to her ankles. There they stayed, since her boots were in the way, but the hindrance would be minor. Shandi waggled her eyebrows. "So you *are* keeping the uniform on. That's just this side of kinky."

Tyra grumble-huffed. "I don't do scenes. We aren't playing enforcer and detainee."

"Yeah, we kinda are." Shandi toyed with a strand that had escaped Tyra's braid.

"The job's not a game." Tyra winced at how stern she sounded. *I'm going to scare her off like this now. Great.*

Shandi kissed her forehead. "Teasing. Sorry. I'll learn what's teasable and what's not."

"It's okay. I... sorry for growling."

Tempting to dive right in, but Tyra made herself lean back to take in a mostly naked Shandi, her shirt rucked up over compact breasts, her economical curves exposed. Her hands circled a good bit of

Shandi's waist as she leaned forward and sucked on one brown nipple while Shandi hummed her approval. Her fingers tightened in Tyra's hair, and the thought flashed by about messing up her braid at work, but she flicked the thought away. *You can re-braid it. Later. This first.*

Easing Shandi's thighs farther apart, Tyra licked her way down Shandi's torso until she reached the top of the dark nest of curls at the bottom. There, she stopped again to look and breathe in Shandi's excitement, a lovely, heady spice. As she slid off her chair to her knees, she ran her thumbs down the outsides of Shandi's labia. The shiver she got in response encouraged her and made her squirm a bit herself. Shandi was so responsive to touch that there wasn't any question what she enjoyed.

She moved her thumbs inward, stroking gently, parting the folds to reveal her target. Shandi wriggled closer, fingers buried in Tyra's hair, grab claw fastened on the edge of the desk as if she might fly off otherwise—and wasn't that a little ego boost? Tyra hadn't even touched her hot button yet.

Always stroking downward, Tyra continued toward the center, parting the inner lips gently. When the scent of excitement wrapped around her and Shandi's pussy glistened, Tyra leaned in to take Shandi's clit between her teeth.

"Holy fuck! Tyra!" Shandi's grip on her hair tightened to near painful, hips bucking up toward Tyra.

In answer, she closed her lips around the nub

and sucked, tongue flicking rhythmically against it. Shandi's words had eroded into desperate sounds of pleasure, her thighs tightening in a heated embrace around Tyra. When she eased the pad of her thumb just inside, Shandi's hips arched off the desk, and she cried out, pussy clenching hard around Tyra's thumb.

The cries softened into little sighs, and Tyra pulled back, just remembering in time not to wipe her mouth on her uniform sleeve.

Shandi smiled down at her, eyes raking up and down. "Either it's been longer than I thought or you're very good. Or both. I'm going with both."

"I should..." Tyra blushed under the weight of that sensual gaze. "Let you get yourself back together."

"Really?" Shandi's smile slipped into concern. "You don't want me to return the favor?"

Of course she did, but she wasn't sure of her own reactions, and she didn't want to push. "I..."

Shandi's grab claw closed on the front of Tyra's jacket. "C'mere and stop thinking so hard."

Flailing, Tyra caught her balance on the edge of the desk as Shandi pulled her up. What if she couldn't? What if she whited out in the middle of things? What if she panicked so badly she couldn't breathe, and in turn, panicked Shandi? What if... Then Shandi was kissing her and pushing her onto her back on the desk. The *what ifs* faded to frightened whispers under the melting heat of Shandi's lips.

Fumbling with Tyra's belt, Shandi shifted to straddle her, and Tyra didn't need to be cudgeled over the head with hints. She undid the belt and fastenings of her pants and shoved both them and her underwear down to her knees.

"You all right still?" Shandi stroked the side of her face, hands stilled as she waited for an answer.

She asked the question seriously, so Tyra took a moment to be sure. Clear, present, and getting a little desperate. "Yes."

"I won't do anything you don't want, and you say stop any time—"

"Shandi." Tyra fought against grinding her teeth. "Gods' sakes. Yes. Please."

The smile returned, that glorious smile, and Shandi lowered herself to lie beside Tyra, her grab claw still clutching the front of Tyra's jacket. She nuzzled behind Tyra's ear and caressed the inside of Tyra's thigh with her nonmetal hand.

Tyra wrapped an arm around her and scooted them away from the desk's control panel. The last thing she needed was to accidentally call one of her staff or unlock the door, or oceans forbid, set off an alarm. Once her hand was against Shandi's back, she had no desire to move it. She stroked up and down the sleek, hard muscles, probably maintained without the two hours daily gym regimen Tyra needed, since Shandi's job didn't involve sitting behind a desk.

"I need to move down. You're too tall." Shandi followed words with action and left off nuzzling

Tyra's ear in favor of burying her face between Tyra's breasts. She didn't seem to care that she'd probably have button marks on her face from the jacket.

Thoughts of buttons and fitness regimens flew out of Tyra's head when Shandi's clever fingers slid between her folds. Thumb stroking lightly over Tyra's clit, Shandi's first two digits teased at her entrance, spreading the wetness already there before sliding inside.

A flaming sun blossomed between her thighs, and Tyra barely had time to gasp and let her breath out on a shuddering moan when Shandi began to move. Thumb and fingers pressed inward together, deeper with each thrust in a gentle, inescapable rhythm. Every stroke increased the delicious tightening inside. Tyra held on tight, a distant realization whispering past her delight-soaked brain about how long it had been.

Her hips rolling in time to Shandi's fingers, Tyra clamped her jaw shut to stifle her shout of pleasure as her orgasm supernovaed, her walls clamping down hard on Shandi again and again. Shandi gentled her movements and finally stilled, bringing Tyra expertly back down before she withdrew her hand.

Tyra lay panting, pressing Shandi tight against her. This had worked, despite all of her anxieties about letting someone so close again. It had *worked*. "I, ah, can't promise it'll always... I mean, that I'll get all the way through."

"What?" Shandi lifted her head, her forehead creased. "Oh, you mean without interruptions or maybe at all. Look, I'm not so demanding I can't stop if you need to. You just say. Anytime. It's not like I expect you to change just 'cause I'm your..."

Shandi trailed off, though Tyra had no difficulty following her line of thought. "Yes. What *are* we now?"

"Guess it's too early to say partners. Or even girlfriend, huh?"

"Maybe a little."

"How about this, then?" Shandi hitched herself back up along Tyra's body until they were nose to nose. "Friends who save each other from monsters with the option for benefits."

Tyra couldn't help a snicker. "That's a mouthful. Friends, yes. I'm your friend."

"One step at a time, Major." Shandi reached up and booped Tyra's nose with her grab claw. "I'm definitely here for that."

"Speaking of here." Tyra sat up carefully so she wouldn't knock Shandi off the desk. "I'd like you here when Endra Fi comes. The trainer the ambassador sent."

Shandi slid off the desk to get her clothes back on properly. "Moral support?"

"You had the first-stage chep. Kif might have questions."

"All right." Those two words weren't sure and certain at all. "And you'll protect me if kif wants to bite my head off?"

"I don't think—"

"No, no, the correct answer is..." Shandi put her hands on her hips and stood on tiptoe as she deepened her voice. "Yes, Shandi. I will protect you from all chep trainers and accountants."

Tyra sputtered, and the laugh got away from her until her eyes watered. Shandi's impression of her as a melodramatic vid hero was just too ridiculous. When she could breathe again, she managed, "Right. No violence in my office. Against regs."

With a gusty sigh, Shandi collapsed into the chair beside Tyra's desk. "Good thing, since I'm trying never, ever to break another regulation again."

Another laugh surprised Tyra, and she couldn't remember the last day she'd laughed so much. They'd call it friends for now, but the warm embers around Tyra's heart said they both knew it was already more.

CHAPTER FIVE

THE KLTRA TRANSPORT'S approach gave
Shandi enough time to go back to her apartment for
a shower and a change of clothes. She had no idea
how good kltra scent was, but she spent her days
with nonhumans and knew the scent of human sex
wasn't anywhere close to subtle.

She thought about starting to pack up, since even
before meeting with Uwe Menotti, she knew there
wasn't any way she could keep the place. Back to
crew quarters she went, where she hadn't lived since
she'd been a young apprentice mechanic. Back to no
personal space and no privacy in the showers. *Not
the end of the world, but discouraging?
Demoralizing? Yeah. Those.*

Regret over the imminent loss of living space
was the least of the volatile feelings doing meteor-
strike crashes through her system.

Stupid chep, ruining her good arm. Though
Shandi acknowledged she really couldn't blame

anyone but herself. She'd have to get someone else to do all the fine motor work for now, and while Teg was more than capable, it didn't sit right with her to have someone else doing the work. The rest of the money worries she couldn't even get her brain around yet. The problem was too huge.

Major Tyra Sur had not only *not* yelled at her but had been helpful and sympathetic and, merciful gods, had sex with Shandi in her office—*on her desk.* And she said they were friends, though the way Tyra said it, soft and shy, sounded to Shandi like she already considered them more. *Progress!*

Anxiety over meeting with the chep trainer threatened to overwhelm everything else. Kltra were generally reasonable people, but they had a violent history to rival humans, and sometimes, even members of the most civilized species could overreact. Those *beaks...*

No sense getting back into work clothes, since her work cycle was long over. Instead, Shandi poured herself into a pair of black synth-leather pants—for Tyra—a blue, long-sleeved T-shirt—for comfort—and a gray vest with various pockets so she might look semiprofessional for their kltra visitor.

With a little sigh, she patted the ruins of the chep's container and headed back to Tyra's office in Biological Customs. A horrific shriek reached her when she'd got to the hallway outside and set her sprinting into the office, visions of blood and catastrophe in her head.

She pounded the door pad, squeezed through at the barest opening, and stood panting in the doorway. Tyra stood at her desk, arms folded, looking stern but not in distress. A red-and-silver kltra in a flowing skirt and half-cape of gray-speckled cream stared at kif's hand-screen, bright crest raised and trembling in anger. No blood, no dismemberment or escaped chep, but the tension in the air crackled and spat.

Tyra held up a hand to keep Shandi where she was. "Problem, Endra Fi?"

Kif's thick beak, powerful enough to take off a human leg, clacked twice. "Genetic registry shows this stolen from the Flock Harbinger's own stock."

The anxiety in Shandi's stomach increased to a dark-star mass threatening to pull her through the floor. Her ussi—chep—came from cheps owned by the United Kltra Federation's high commander. This was bad, so bad.

"I'm sorry," Shandi blurted out, even though Tyra's eye roll made it clear she should have been quiet. "I didn't know. I didn't even know it was a chep. I'll make whatever restitution needs to be made."

Endra Fi turned slowly, kif's clawed feet kneading the carpet in what Shandi thought was a menacing way. "Restitution for such an offense would be death."

Shandi couldn't keep her feet from backing away. "Oh. Um..."

"Endra Fi." Tyra stepped between them, calm

and professional. "This is Chief Leavenworth, who was duped into the purchase."

Kif's crest lowered as Endra Fi inclined kif's head, though the crest didn't seem to want to stay down, springing up and lowering several more times. "Shocking—this crime. The thief will answer, though, not you. Kltra enforcement searches for him now."

"So *Alain's* going to die?" Shandi didn't have any good feelings about Teg's former friend, but she didn't want him executed.

"Perhaps." Endra Fi waved a feathered hand. "Humans will speak for him. Negotiation. Mitigation. Who can say?"

"Again, the sincere apologies of this station and its staff, Endra Fi." Tyra sounded like she was picking up the conversation from before the screech. "Will you be taking the chep? Since it's royal?"

Kif let out a little *creeee-eek*, which could've been irritation or it could've been a thinking sound. "Flock Harbinger will be told. We do *not* recommend taking chep from their metamorphosis environment."

"Ah..." Tyra paled, obviously reaching the conclusion Shandi had. "You suggest we *keep* it? Endra Fi, we don't have any experience—"

Click-click-click. The beak cut her off. "I will remain for training. Late, yes. But chep are intelligent beings. Even now, it can learn."

"What would it learn?" Shandi found she'd drifted closer, curiosity overcoming fear.

"Usefulness. Helpfulness. To not eat hatchlings. Acceptable food." Endra Fi looked down kif's beak at Shandi. "A great honor, to be on the rolls as owner of one of its bloodline."

"Oh, no. No, no, no." Shandi waved one hand over the other in negation. "Not me. I bought the chep for Major Sur."

Tyra shot her a glare that could've brought down a dreadnought, but Endra Fi's crest stayed down, kif's eyes widening.

"Ah! Gifted to a warrior. Yes, Major Sur. You will keep the chep. It is yours."

Hand on her heart, Tyra offered a bow. "Honored, Endra Fi."

"Yes." Kif tucked her data pad into a hidden skirt pocket and clacked kif's beak. "A secure room and seven work cycles. Also food. What was first life cycle fed?"

Shandi tried not to cringe, wondering how wrong she'd been. "Um, mostly kale chips."

"I believe kale is vegetative." Endra Fi nodded, feathers swaying. "Well done, Chief Leavenworth."

"You're welcome to one of the holding cells." Tyra bent to hit the comm on her desk. "Agitou, could you come in and bring a cart?" After a moment's hesitation, she added, "And a box of kale chips?"

Agitou's voice implied doubts of Tyra's sanity. "Kale chips, Major?"

"For the chep." Tyra cut the connection and

straightened. "We're grateful, Endra Fi. Please let us know if you need anything during your stay."

Once Agitou had manhandled the chep's container onto his float cart and led Endra Fi away, Tyra sank into her desk chair, scrubbing both hands over her face.

"Hey. You okay?" Shandi hoisted herself onto the desk beside Tyra, getting inappropriate but delicious *déjà vu* images when she wriggled her way onto the surface.

"Am I okay?" Tyra muttered into her hands. "I'm now the proud owner of a deadly royal pudding."

"Um, Happy Solstice?"

Tyra snorted but lifted her head. "Well, we'll figure it out. Endra Fi comes highly recommended, though."

"So you're saying if anyone can civilize our chep run amok, it's kif." Shandi heaved a sigh, half weary and half relieved. "Should I apologize again?"

"I don't know. I haven't kept track."

"Ha! A joke." Shandi poked the braid on Tyra's uniform sleeve.

"I should ask for one for pointing to me as the owner." Tyra took her hand and made no sign of letting go. "But kif seemed pleased. I guess it's better this way."

"Because it was a present?"

"No, because I have more experience with weird pets." Tyra took Shandi's hand in both of hers, expression serious again. "Shandi, I..."

Uh-oh. Is this the we can't see each other

anymore *talk*? "You can tell me. Whatever it is. I'm still your friend no matter what, okay?" To her own surprise, Shandi realized she meant it.

Tyra huffed a breath, staring at their joined hands. "I don't want you to be... offended. Or think I'm trying to... to push you. But if you need to give up your apartment. If you need a place..."

"I'm seeing your trajectory here, but keep going."

"My apartment's a good size. You could, ah, move in with me?"

Shandi leaned forward to kiss Tyra's forehead. "That's incredibly generous, and I appreciate it. You sure you'd be okay with someone in your space, though?"

Slowly, Tyra lifted her head, her eyes shining as she met Shandi's. "I would if the someone was you."

"Sweet-talker." Shandi curled over to plant a gentle kiss on her lips. "I'm not offended at all. If I'm homeless, I'm holding you to this. And if it gets too much or you want your space back, you just say. Promise?"

"I promise." Tyra stood and stretched her back. "Long day. Want to come home with me and practice?"

Shandi gave her a full-wattage smile. "I thought you'd never ask."

⊙

ENDRA FI'S promised seven days turned into ten, since once kif deemed the chep sufficiently trained,

Tyra had to be trained on chep care and handling. Kif had also insisted that Tyra name the chep. To her embarrassment, she'd blurted out "Ussi Pudding," which Endra Fi promptly listed in the royal registry.

It turned out Ussi wasn't so different from Tyra in many ways. The chep liked routine and predictability. It attached to one or two people, but did so with all its metaphorical heart. Stress and metamorphosis hunger had made their chep feral, but that wasn't its normal state.

"If Flock Harbinger wishes to breed this line, I will return." Endra Fi's statement held a note of warning as kif prepared to board the transport back to the kltra home world. "With others."

"Ah. Well." Tyra offered a little bow. "We look forward to your possible visit."

With a ruffle of feathers and a beak clack, Endra Fi turned in a swirl of diaphanous fabric and left the station, both diplomatic and faunal crises resolved. Tyra went back to her office with Ussi undulating soundlessly along at her side, peacefully avoiding anyone they passed.

"Attachep," Tyra patted an extended pseudopod when they entered her office and gave Ussi a kale chip for behaving so well. Ussi settled beside Tyra's desk in a roughly circular mound, content to sleep or rest or whatever it did while Tyra worked.

Several permit approvals waited for her yes or no. A diplomat passing through with what amounted to a pet dire caterpillar threatened to cause an issue later that morning. Nothing alarming or out of the ordinary looming, at least not until that evening after work cycle.

A celebration loomed. To make matters worse, Tyra had been the one to suggest it.

Shandi had agreed officially to share Tyra's apartment. Life and Health Services had assisted in every way they could—negotiating totals for damages, setting up payment agreements, helping her find the right organization for a prosthetic replacement monetary fund—but her apartment wouldn't fit into the plan, no matter how Uwe had juggled the figures.

It had been a definite blow to Shandi's pride. Even though she tried to joke about it, Tyra couldn't miss the tightening of her jaw, the hurt in her eyes at losing something she had worked hard for. Tyra hadn't pushed, but she'd encouraged Shandi's staying with her more and more, and by the end of the week, most of Shandi's belongings had migrated to Tyra's place. It wasn't perfect. She would've been worried if it was. Tyra grumbled about the strange odds and ends Shandi felt she needed to keep. Shandi fussed about what she called Tyra's "abandoned apartment aesthetic."

On the other hand, it was wonderful to have someone to talk to besides her own glitchy brain, to have someone to hold onto after night terrors, and even Shandi's bad habits were endearing ones. Tyra had become more and more certain this would work, so they'd signed the official contract for a joint apartment that morning, which prompted the idea of a moving-in-day celebration.

Which, of course, means I have to go. Saying, "Hey, let's invite everyone to celebrate with us" and then following up with, "I don't feel like attending" doesn't sound remotely reasonable or sane. How did that suggestion even spill out of my mouth?

Some of Shandi's overpowering optimism spilling over, most likely. Tyra would have to watch out for that. She wasn't comfortable with spontaneous decisions.

The work cycle raced by, culminating in Tyra having to insist that the magachan ambassador leave her horse-sized caterpillar on her ship. The ambassador was annoyed but became more understanding when she walked through some of the station's corridors and understood how narrow they were.

With the last permit processed, Tyra had run out of excuses. She rose from her desk. "Come on, Ussi. We can be social for a while. We don't have to stay long."

A pseudopod popped up out of the mound to simulate a head, and Ussi glided obediently after her. During the walk to La Luna, Ussi only butted Tyra's pocket once to ask for treats. The chep really was trying to be good.

At the door, Tyra hesitated, and Ussi pressed up against her legs as if it sensed her unease. The corner of the bar pulled at her. She wanted so badly to go to her corner and at least have the illusion of hiding.

But they were supposed to have a table, and the chances of her having arrived first were slim to none. ...

"Major!"

Tyra turned to see Dr. Emilia waving from across the room where, yes, everyone had already gathered. Oh. They'd all changed out of their coveralls and uniforms. Tyra was the only one coming directly from work. The temptation to turn around and pretend she hadn't seen them was nearly overwhelming. So many people in the bar that evening. But there was Shandi, batting Dr. Emilia's waving tail out of her face and smiling bright enough to shame the stars.

So Tyra chose forward instead of back.

Limp-bouncing, Miteg hurried over to greet her, spotted Ussi with a startled squeak, and leap-flapped away to the top of a chair, which promptly tipped over. Most likely anticipating disaster, Agitou was there to catch him before he hit the floor.

Ussi's pseudopod swiveled back and forth between Tyra and Miteg as if the chep was unsure.

"I'm sure Ussi would say sorry if she could." Tyra stroked the offered faux-head.

"You all right, Teg?" Shandi jogged over as Agitou put Miteg back on his feet. "You're supposed to have that leg up after work. And you know Ussi's not going to hurt you. Um, not again, anyway."

Still Miteg had inched behind her. "It startled me. That's all. Startled. Not that I see it in my nightmares or anything."

Clara took one of Miteg's hands, and Agitou still had another as she turned them back toward the table. "Come sit down, Teg. Food'll be here any second."

Apparently, Miteg was more food-motivated than Ussi, since he immediately limp-skipped back to the table, trauma forgotten. And since when were Tyra's staff on a nickname basis with him? *Interesting.*

A few deep, counted breaths later, Tyra had crossed the restaurant full of staring eyes and taken her seat between Shandi and Dr. Emilia. Shandi took her hand, and some of the rising panic receded, replaced by the feeling of having reached an island of security in an uncertain place. It helped that Tyra's back was to the wall.

Service staff soon brought huge bowls of ramen, a food they could all agree on as long as everyone had their own bowls of additions—pickled fish for Dr. Emilia, tofu for the humans, red grubs for Miteg, and something gelatinous and wobbly for Agitou that Tyra didn't want to think about too hard.

Conversation came in short spurts, with everyone busy slurping noodles, and Tyra felt some of her tension melting into the floor.

"Ussi looks good, Major." Dr. Emilia stroked a red-furred hand over the chep's pseudopod. "How was behavior today?"

"Excellent. Still settling in with regular food times. Little bit of begging for snacks. But a good chep today."

A clicking rattle from Tyra's left pulled her attention to where Miteg, despite having four hands, had managed to drop his sticks on the floor. Ussi dove for them to the accompaniment of several gasps around the table and Miteg's alarmed squeak. But Tyra sat still, waiting. With a finger-like pseudopod, Ussi retrieved the sticks from the floor and held them up to Miteg. He took them gingerly with a faint *thank-you*.

"Good chep." Tyra offered pets when Ussi returned to her and gave her a kale chip reward.

Shandi raised an eyebrow at her. "Wow. How... I mean... Ussi can tell when something's dropped food or not?"

"There's a command." Tyra cleared her throat when she realized everyone had focused on her. "If it's dropped food to clean up, you have to say so. If not, Ussi will hand, ah, give it back."

Miteg still held his sticks between one clawed thumb and forefinger as if they might bite him. "Is it okay to use them? After the chep held, um, gripped... puddinged them?"

"Teg." Dr. Emilia snagged a new pair for him from the table's center caddy. "Don't you think you should be more worried about them being on the floor? And no, I wouldn't recommend it."

There were snickers and snorts, but Miteg took it all in good humor and went back to devouring his food. Ussi snuggled back up against Tyra's leg.

"Thanks for coming, everyone." Shandi lifted her cup with a grin. "To the new apartment contract."

The nonhumans had been around humans long enough to know this ritual. Everyone clinked drinking vessels with Shandi, and answering murmurs with some variation of *apartment* and *contract* ran around the table.

Dr. Emilia's ears swiveled back and forth. "So, will you be getting married soon? I'm certified to officiate in seventeen different species ceremonies."

"Oh, I *love* weddings," Clara sighed. "Especially cake."

"Silliness," Agitou grumbled. "Should just spawn like normal people."

Miteg nudged Shandi with an elbow. "Nesting. I'm telling you. Nothing like it."

Taken completely off guard, Tyra found herself unable to respond. All of her brain cells had ossified.

"Hey, let's not rush." Shandi laughed, and the sound sluiced over Tyra's raw confusion. "Let's see if the major wants to kick me out after three months first. And no one wants to marry someone as buried in debt as I am. Couple years, though, when I'm more solvent—who knows? One thing at a time."

A couple of years... Shandi was looking at this as long-term. Looking toward the future, one that included *together*. Tyra glanced around the table and down at the shining purple creature nuzzling her boots and realized she wasn't solitary any longer. She had people to trust, people who had her back, who cared whether she was happy.

She took Shandi's chin in her fingers and turned her face for a searing kiss in front of the gods, their friends, and the entire bar. Heat rushed up her face in a deep blush, but her heart wasn't trying to leap out of her chest in a panic, and the warmth at her core came from more than just the promise in that kiss.

Family. This was family, maybe a little untraditional, but that didn't matter.

"One thing at a time," she said as she gazed into Shandi's dark, laughing eyes. "But forward. Always forward."

DEAR READER

Thank you for purchasing Angel Martinez's **The Solstice Pudding.** We hope you enjoyed it as much as we did. We hope you will consider leaving a review wherever you purchased this ebook and/or on Goodreads. Reviews and word-of-mouth recommendations are *vital* to independent publishers.

If you enjoyed this story by Angel, then you may also enjoy her story, *Safety Protocols for Human Holidays,* or you may want to explore Freddy MacKay's, *Waiting on the Rain.*

We love hearing from our readers. You can email us at mischiefcornerbooks@gmail.com. To read excerpts from all our titles, visit our website: http://www.mischiefcornerbooks.com.

Sincerely,
    Mischief Corner Books

YOU MAY ALSO ENJOY...

www.mischiefcornerbooks.com

YOU MAY ALSO ENJOY...

www.mischiefcornerbooks.com

YOU MAY ALSO ENJOY...

www.mischiefcornerbooks.com

YOU MAY ALSO ENJOY...

www.mischiefcornerbooks.com

ABOUT ANGEL MARTINEZ

While Angel Martinez is the erotic fiction pen name
of a writer of several genres, she writes both kinds of
gay romance – Science Fiction and Fantasy.
Currently living part time in the hectic sprawl of
northern Delaware, (and full time inside the author's
head) Angel has one husband, one son, two cats, a
changing variety of other furred and scaled
companions, a love of all things beautiful and a
terrible addiction to the consumption of both
knowledge and chocolate.

For more information on Angel's work, please
visit:

Official Website:
http://angelmartinezauthor.weebly.com/

Email:
angelmartinezauthor@gmail.com

facebook.com/Angel.Martinez.author

twitter.com/AngelMartinezrr

ALSO BY ANGEL MARTINEZ

Safety Protocols for Human Holidays

Yule Planet

The Solstice Pudding

BRANDYWINE INVESTIGATIONS

Brandywine Investigations: Open for Business (Omnibus)

Brandywine Investigations: Family Matters (Omnibus)

BRIMSTONE

Potato Surprise #1

Hell for the Company #2

Fear of Frogs #3

Shax's War #4

Beside a Black Tarn #5

The Hunt for Red Fluffy #6

The Brimstone Journals: Collection One

The Brimstone Journals: Collection Two

THE ENDANGERED FAE SERIES

Finn

Diego

Semper Fae

No Fae is an Island

ESTO UNIVERSE

Vassily the Beautiful

Prisoner 374215

A Matter of Faces

Gravitational Attraction

LIJUN Trilogy (with Freddy Mackay)

Fireworks & Stolen Kisses

Trysts & Burning Embers

Detonations & Devotion (TBD)

INTERPLANETARY MULTISPECIES PACT (IMP)

A Christmas Cactus for the General

A Message from the Home Office*

*Currently awaiting republication

THE WEB OF ARCANA

The Mage on the Hill

OFFBEAT CRIMES

Lime Gelatin and Other Monsters

Pill Bugs of Time

Skim Blood & Savage Verse

Feral Dust Bunnies

Jackalopes & Woofen-Poofs

All the World's an Undead Stage

SINGLE TITLES

The Color of His Crest

Hearts & Flowers: A Tale of Hay Fever and Bad Decor

Restoration

The Line

Meteor Strike: Serge and Een

AURA UNIVERSE (with Bellora Quinn)

Quinn's Gambit

Flax's Pursuit

Kellen's Awakening

ABOUT MISCHIEF CORNER BOOKS

Mischief Corner Books is an organization of superheroes... no, it's a platinum-album techno-fusion group... no, hold on a sec here...

Ah yes. Mischief Corner is a small press publisher offering queer romance and fiction for readers, intent on making some mayhem with our books. Diversity and positive representation for all members of the queer community is important to us, and MCB works to make those voices heard because those who travel the off the beaten path are a gift and their stories make the world a more interesting place.

In addition to making mayhem, we live to break molds. MCB. Giving voice to LGBTQ fiction.

Website:
http://www.mischiefcornerbooks.com

facebook.com/MischiefCorner
twitter.com/MischiefCorner

Made in the USA
Coppell, TX
04 January 2023

10318178R00080